In a Time

Where They

Belong

Brenda Cheers

BIRDCALL PUBLISHING AUSTRALIA

www.brendacheersbooks.com

First Edition

Author image Sargaison / Brisbane Headshots

Cover image © Stacey Newman / iStockphoto.com

ISBN-13: 978-0-9924287-2-3

To every other author trying to weave magic—
may the words flow as fast as the mightiest river.

Also by Brenda Cheers:

In Times of Trouble

In Conversations with Strangers

In a House in Yemen

In Strange Worlds

In a Time Where They Belong

Brenda Cheers

Maleny is a small town 90 kilometres (56 miles) north of Brisbane. Its population before the events of May 2013 was approximately 2,500.

PROLOGUE

She is with him now, his Sophie, returned to him by the call of a bird that mimicked the pitch of her laughter exactly. She sits beside him, murmuring soft words. He is complete.

She is gone again, suddenly, just like everyone else he knew before May 13th. He empties, crumbles. He is alone in this strange world, frightened and suicidal.

Just as he feels he cannot bear it anymore—that he can no longer go on—she is with him again, returned by the scent of a flower that mimicked the perfume she always wore.

CHAPTER ONE

"It's just too damned hot for this!"

Heather blew some hair from her face and shunted the child over to the other hip. She looked at George, but he just shrugged and lifted the other twin into the air, smiling as the boy giggled.

"You wouldn't be so relaxed if you were pregnant!"

"No, but I'd be a miracle man!"

Derek smiled at George's humour and his ability to deflect Heather's negativity. "You would indeed, mate. Let's all take a break for a few minutes."

Heather sank onto the road with a groan. "My feet are so swollen I don't think I can walk much further."

Derek turned to see how India and John were coping. They each had a child strapped to the front of their torsos and a backpack at the rear. They were walking easily, and John was talking and pointing with enthusiasm. Derek knew he'd be telling India about the ecology of the area. As the couple drew closer, they slowed.

"Taking a break? I think we'd rather just keep walking. How far now?" John's smile was disarming.

Derek checked the sun's position before unfolding the map. "Mate, I reckon we'll be able to see the hill when we go around the next bend. Probably only half an hour."

John looked at India who smiled and kept walking. "Too hard to unstrap everything. We'll just walk slowly."

"Okay, but the turn-off is to the right, just past the bend. You'll see the house on the hill, to the left. Wait for me at the end of the driveway."

John waved and fell into a stride that matched India's. The others could hear his commentary fading into the distance.

Derek crouched and inspected Heather's right foot. He pressed on the skin and saw the indentation left behind. "A bit of fluid retention, but nothing too serious. Meg or Connie will make you a foot-bath."

"I'm worried about them. They don't know we're coming. What if they don't want us there?"

"It won't be a problem. They'll just be excited to discover more survivors." Derek looked at George and raised his eyebrows. George got the hint.

"C'mon Heather. Not far now. I'll help you up." He held out his arms, and Heather levered herself vertical. The two of them took a few minutes to arrange themselves and the children again, before resuming their slow walk.

Derek turned full circle to take in the lush landscape. He'd forgotten how magical the Maleny area was, especially the sweet, fresh air. He tuned into the sounds around him and tried to determine individual bird calls, but there were too many.

It had looked easy on the map, the walk from Noosaville to Meg's house. In a car it would only have taken an hour. There had been several unsuccessful attempts at finding a suitable vehicle—it had to be unlocked, have the keys, have fuel, and be mechanically sound—but time had taken its toll on machinery. The one vehicle they found only lasted ten kilometres, but at least that cut the journey by an eighth.

They rounded the bend. Derek jogged forward and turned into the road on the right. He darted one way, then another, trying to see through the trees. "I see it!" He ran back to Heather and George. "I see the house! Not far now."

Heather gave a small smile. "Thank heavens. It's all uphill, though."

"Give me Stephanie. I can carry her."

"Are you sure? You've already got a lot of our stuff. What about your back?"

"I'm sure. I really want to get there now. I'm looking forward to seeing Meg again. Luke and Connie, too."

They strode in silence. Derek didn't mind carrying Stephanie, her relaxed body spread over his chest, one arm around his neck and the other near her mouth. He could hear her sucking a thumb.

John and India came into view. They were still standing, and their position was one of relaxed anticipation.

Derek passed Stephanie back to Heather and jogged up to the gate, remembering how he had helped Meg attach it to the fence-posts they'd sunk. It still looked good. He undid the chain and swung the gate inward, finding the brick they used to hold it open. "I'll go ahead and tell Meg we're here!" He ran up the driveway shouting, "Meg! Meg!"

A figure came around the side of the verandah. As he came closer he saw it wasn't Meg, but Connie.

"Derek? Is that really you?" She clasped her hands together. "How wonderful!"

"And I've brought others with me. Look!"

Connie's eyes grew wide as she saw the other four adults, each carrying a child. "Oh, Derek. Another eight of us alive. Where did you find them?"

"They found me. I had to help with the kids' health, but they're pretty good now. I thought this would be the best place for them."

"Yes, yes. Of course. I'll go and introduce myself..."

Derek began walking toward the glass door that led into the back of the house. "Meg! Meg!" Luke came out of one of the sheds, wiping dirty hands on his overalls. He saw Derek and began running toward him.

"Oh, wow. Derek. So good to see you!"

"You can talk!"

Luke reddened. "Yeah. A while ago now. And we've got two more kids." He smiled. "What's been happening?"

"I've been collecting people. Look!"

Derek enjoyed watching the look of astonishment cross the younger man's face as he took in the people walking up to Connie. "Are they better than the last lot you brought here?"

"Yeah, mate. All good people."

"That's a relief."

"I reckon this would be the place for them."

"Yeah, of course."

Derek felt impatience rising. "I still haven't seen Meg."

Luke's face dropped. "Connie didn't tell you?"

"No, what?" He felt his heart skip a beat.

The younger man looked down at his feet. "She..."

"What?"

"She's gone."

"Gone? Where?"

"Under the big tree. We buried her there. She wanted that."

Derek stared at Luke for several moments. Comprehension came slowly. There was the misunderstanding, then the denial, then the sadness. Always the sadness. He closed his eyes. Not again. He couldn't stand the sadness all over again.

When Derek opened his eyes Connie was walking toward the two of them, with the four adults bringing up the rear.

"Are you okay?" Luke was looking at him with a worried expression.

Derek filled his lungs and let the breath out with a rush. "Yeah, mate. Just a bit of a shock. Let's get these guys sorted." He looked at Connie. "We'll get Heather into the reclining chair. If you can arrange a foot-bath, I'll make her a cold drink."

"Okay. C'mon Heather. Let's get you comfortable. When are you due? I suppose it's twins again?"

The women kept chatting as they moved into the house. Derek motioned to the other to follow and then looked over at the big tree. Later. He needed to be strong now. Straightening his shoulders, he crossed into the dim living room.

"Meg saw this, you know." Connie was leaning forward, speaking softly to Derek.

"Saw what?"

"Just before she died. Said that if this was a movie with a happy ending, it would show you coming back, leading a group of adults and children. She could see us sitting at that table out the front, watching you all come up the driveway."

Derek nodded.

"She was very fond of you, you know." Connie lifted her blouse and began feeding the baby on her lap. "Disappointed when you left."

"Yeah, I guess that wasn't very nice. So when did she die?"

"Only a week and a bit ago."

"What caused it?"

"That's the thing. It's such a shame you didn't get here earlier—you might have been able to save her."

"From what?"

"Childbirth."

"Hey?" Derek frowned.

"Childbirth. Trying to have twins."

"But..."

"What?"

"I don't understand. Was Luke the father?"

Connie looked at him and blinked. "Luke. Could you come here a minute?"

Luke disengaged from conversation with George. "Yeah. What's up?"

"Derek is asking who the father of the twins was."

Luke frowned and looked at Derek. "You know. When you came back here after the cyclone—"

"What do you mean?"

"After the cyclone—"

"I wasn't here after the cyclone."

"Yes you were. Wasn't he, Connie?"

Connie nodded. "You were acting very strange though."

"That's nonsense! I haven't been back since we finished the fence."

The young couple were staring at him. They seemed to be at a loss for words.

"Okay. Well tell me what I did when I came back, supposedly. You say I was acting strangely."

"Yeah. Really cold and you didn't talk, and Meg said you walked funny."

"You didn't see me walk?"

They shook their heads.

"But you did see me——you didn't just take Meg's word I was here?"

"We helped look after you. Carried you up the hill."

Derek looked around the room. Heather's feet were in a red tub, and she was smiling at her son, Michael, who was holding up a book. George was bouncing Stephanie in his arms while running his palms over the interior walls of the house. John and India were visible through the windows, inspecting the chickens.

"Okay. It seems I was here without knowing it. I impregnated Meg. She was carrying twins but died in childbirth. How about the children?"

Connie's eyes were filling with tears. "Dead. We couldn't save them." She began sobbing. "It was just awful, Derek. You've got no idea!"

Luke had turned away, but Derek could see him wiping his eyes. Derek's own eyes began welling in sympathy. He excused himself and went outside.

John, India and their children were still at the chicken enclosure. Wanting to avoid them, Derek turned to his left and came across a large, tented structure that he had never seen before.

Walking toward it he could see a generator and other machinery. He passed through an entry and saw that it led to a well-equipped operating theatre. Another room had chairs and tables. There were cabinets filled with medicines and first-aid supplies.

Derek scratched his head. Where could this possibly have sprung from?

"The guys in the helicopter put it here." Luke had walked in quietly and surprised the older man. "Sorry if we upset you back there."

"It's okay mate. I'll have to accept the fact I was here but didn't know it. More importantly—what helicopter guys?"

"The ones that came to save Meg. But they crashed."

Luke spent the next half hour explaining everything to Derek. "The worst part was that there was someone in the helicopter with them. Maybe he would have been able to explain a whole lotta stuff."

"Indeed. That trip you did—to the hospital in the desert..."

"Yeah?"

"I was there, or somewhere just like it. That's where I was just after the cyclone. A sheet of roofing got me..."

"You were injured?"

"Yeah, mate. I woke in this strange place, in this dormitory type room with high windows. When I stood on a chair and looked out, all I could see was flat, scrubby land."

"Sounds like the same place."

"I was kept locked up and they passed food in on trays through a slot."

"Really bad food?"

"Yeah. Awful. They must've drugged me when it was time to go. Woke up back at my place at Noosaville."

"Wow."

"I'm impressed by this set-up, though." He waved his arms around. "First class. So, where are the three bodies from the helicopter buried?"

Luke looked at his shoes. "Um...I haven't buried them yet. It was madness——the birth and Meg dying..."

"Yeah, I understand. So where are they?"

"Still at the helicopter. Meg made me go back with a tarp and cover them over."

"What could you see of the third person?"

"Well, there was a huge explosion..."

"Nothing much left?"

"Nup."

"Where is it?"

"Halfway between here and Meg's place."

"Meg's?"

"Oh, you wouldn't know. She found her own place. It's not far."

"The four-wheel-drive——it's still running?"

"Yeah."

"Gas?"

"Yeah."

"Let's go."

As they navigated the dirt roads, Derek enjoyed being behind the wheel. "I'm amazed that Meg found a way of getting the petrol from underground tanks. Having a car makes all the difference."

"Yeah, and this one has dual tanks, so I don't have to fill them too often. Here is the house, on the left."

Derek braked suddenly and slid into the driveway. His first impression of the house and property was favourable. The house was well-positioned, high and facing northeast. There were outbuildings and a dam, water tanks, and solar panels.

When they entered the house, Derek whistled. Marble bench tops, European appliances, timber floors and a view over the Glasshouse Mountains. Wonderful.

"Okay, this is me. I'm moving in here and Heather and

George can have Meg's old room at your place." He rubbed his hands together.

"Yeah, that's cool. That'll work."

"Where did Meg keep her journals? I saw how she used to keep records when I was living there."

"We've buried them."

"Hey? What?"

"That was part of her last wishes. She wanted us to make a sort of time capsule and put them in that. For future generations so they'd know what happened on 13th May '13."

"And you've done that already?"

"Yeah, we buried her first, under the tree she loved, just like she asked. Then we made the time capsule and put stuff in it and buried it outside the library."

"Is that where she said to put it?"

"Yup. I was going to cover it with concrete and put up a sign as well, but I haven't got to that yet."

"Hmm. Okay. Don't just yet. I made a decision today."

"Oh?"

"Yeah. I'm going to find out what happened. I want to know why everyone except us died that night and I want to know who those people are that make us have dreams and help us with medical issues."

"I haven't had any of those weird, vivid dreams since

we rescued Connie from Cairns. Have you?"

"Not since I first came to your place—that must've been near the end of 2014. Right?"

"Dunno. Meg always kept track of dates. She told Connie to start her own journals and record dates and events."

"Smart."

"We miss Meg real bad. You know?"

"Yeah."

"Connie and I kinda thought you two would get together."

"We should have. She'd probably still be alive." He paused. "It was me. I was still too messed up. Probably still am."

"Oh, okay."

"Anyway, as I was saying, I want to get answers. Find out what happened."

"That's going to be hard, you know."

"Doesn't matter. I'm just going to do it. I'll need Meg's journals though. I'll get them tomorrow. After I've read them, I'll put them back. Then I'll concrete it over and make a sign."

"Sure."

"Aren't you curious about what happened back then— why everyone died?"

Luke shrugged.

"I've noticed that. You younger ones are more accepting."

"That's what Meg always said."

Derek looked outside. "It's getting late. We'll go and look at the helicopter tomorrow—perhaps first up in the morning?"

"Sure."

"Then I'll go and get Meg's journals and start reading. Look, there's the perfect spot. See that window-seat? That's where I'll spend tomorrow." He rubbed his hands together and smiled.

Finally the children were fed and put to bed. Connie and Heather had made the formal lounge into a makeshift dormitory and raided cupboards for blankets and pillows. Maisie and Thomas, the two oldest children, had helped as best they could before making their own nests and burrowing down to sleep.

The adults were weary as well, but still needed food and a place to sleep. They were all in the living area talking among themselves when Derek rose and cleared his throat. Everybody quietened.

"It's official—Luke and Connie have agreed that you

can all come and live here. We'll create a community."

Everybody applauded softly. They didn't want to disturb the children.

"This will benefit everybody, including Luke and Connie, who have been feeling a bit lost since Meg's death." There were slow nods around the room. "Every person will be expected to work hard. There will be building projects and farming and childcare duties. There will be cooking and cleaning. We'll draw up a roster in due course."

Heather raised her hand. "Where will we live? This isn't a big house."

"I know. I was about to get to that. We've got a few choices. Luke has a four-wheel-drive that can tow a caravan. We can simply tow a couple of them here, if that's what you decide. Otherwise we can get some tents from a camping store—really good ones. Whichever option you decide on will be only temporary. We'll build some cabins."

John raised his hand. "I reckon a good caravan would be beaut."

"I don't know. I hoped to be in the house." Heather looked at George. He shrugged.

"Actually, you can for the time being, Heather, if that's what you want. I'm going to live up the road. You can have Meg's old room until the babies are born. You'll want your own place once you have four children."

Heather nodded. "Thanks, Derek."

"It also means you can help Connie with domestic duties and the children, seeing as you are right here. Okay?"

"Fine."

He looked at John and India. "For tonight, you two can sleep in the portable hospital if you like. It has its own generator and is quite comfortable. The children will be okay in the house here with the other kids."

"Cool! We'll like that." John smiled at India and squeezed her hand.

"But for now we need to feed ourselves. Sorry we couldn't carry food, Connie."

The young woman looked at all the expectant, hungry faces and smiled. "No problem. Luke and I will find enough for us all."

Food wasn't the most urgent thing on Derek's mind. He was already thinking of the next day when he would view the helicopter crash site and dig up Meg's journals. He wanted answers.

CHAPTER TWO

"So, you're saying the crash happened when?"

Luke squeezed one eye closed. "Um, 18th August." He blew into his hands and stamped his feet.

"Yeah, it's bloody cold. Today must be around 28th August, so these bodies have been here for ten days or so. Help me lift the tarp."

They each went to one end and grasped the covering in the middle. They slid it to the right. A rodent scuttled into the burnt fuselage.

"Hmm. You were right. Not much to see here, particularly when I don't know what I'm looking for."

"One of the weird guys had a chipped front tooth, if that helps."

"Yeah, maybe it will. Thanks."

Derek slid his hands into latex gloves and then bent over the three figures. He moved each one sightly, checking what was underneath before putting them back where he found them.

Luke stamped his feet again. "So what do you reckon?"

"No idea. I'll have to find some reference books. I think the best thing to do is cover them over again and I'll do some research. I don't want to move them just yet."

Derek started circling the crash site, increasing the diameter with each rotation, and keeping his gaze on the grass. Occasionally he'd pick something up, examine it and put it back in place.

"Okay, mate. I can see you're cold. That's enough for today."

Luke smiled gratefully, and both men climbed back into the vehicle. Derek paused before starting the engine.

"I'm going to get to the bottom of this, you know."

"Yeah. Okay."

"For now I'll cook us a hot breakfast back at my place."

As Derek drove Meg's four-wheel-drive down Coral Street to Maleny Library, he realised he was actually in a rare good mood. He had deposited the four adults and four children with Luke and Connie and was able to escape for a few hours. He was also very happy with the house he now lived in, which was close enough to be sociable, but remote enough to ensure some privacy.

He'd had the eight of them—George, John, Heather, India, and the children—staying with him for several weeks. Heather and George had arrived first—knocking on his door in the middle of the night, saying they had come for help. John and India arrived next. They all seemed to have medical issues, adults and children alike, which he tried to help them with.

After he'd managed to stabilise them all, it was decided they should move to Maleny, even Derek. Well, he wasn't absolutely sure he'd stay there, but decided to play it by ear. One thing was certain, he was needed. A paediatrician for all these twins being born was an absolute necessity, and as far as he knew, he was the last paediatrician left on earth. Last doctor, too.

The library was squat with a verandah across the front, its strange yellow colouring making it stand out from the vegetation on either side. There was off-street parking that he drove into, backing up to the building so he could unload the tools he had brought.

He could see the freshly turned earth where Luke had buried the time capsule and attacked it with a shovel. Soon he struck the wooden box that he guessed housed the journals and other matter. He cleared the area around the box and pulled it cleanly from the soil.

Derek made tut-tutting sounds when he saw how badly Luke and Connie had organised the 'capsule'. The thin wooden box wouldn't last long in the ground. The journals were only wrapped in cloth. Everything would be rotting in no time.

He sensed a change in the air and turned. Something was moving down the road, but he wasn't sure what. It seemed like a car, but one that wasn't completely there. It was silent and it rippled—not solid. Like a mirage. Derek blinked a couple of times but it remained the same.

It came to a stop in front of the library, on the street, and Derek could see that it was a car after all—a red one. He could make out a rental company sticker on the back window. It was some sort of sporty model, but a few years old. Yes, he had it now. It was a 2012 model, which didn't make any sense because it was now 2016, and major car rental companies didn't keep their vehicles for that long—usually only twelve months. But hang on, he thought. There haven't been any car rental companies since 2013. His brain had stopped functioning properly.

A figure stepped out from behind the steering wheel. It was a woman, and she seemed oblivious to him. She stood still for a few moments, just looking towards the library. Her features weren't clear and she shimmered like the car.

The figure moved toward the library and began searching the grassy area, kicking tufts where they were uneven. As she came closer, Derek realised he was looking at Meg, and he reacted with a shiver. She kept walking, right on course for the hole he'd just dug. He tried to sound a warning, but the noise that issued from his throat was a croak. He could only watch in horrified fascination as she stepped into the hole.

Except that she didn't. She walked over it as though it was firm ground. For the next few minutes she circled around, still kicking tufts of grass. Sometimes she came within touching distance, but she never saw him. Finally, she walked back to the car and drove away.

Derek didn't move for the next few minutes. His mind was trying to make sense of what his eyes had just seen. Meg had been dressed in clothes he'd never seen her wearing before. Her hair was long and straighter than it had been when he stayed with her at Maleny.

He was a man of science—he didn't believe in ghosts. What had he just seen, then?

He eventually found he could move again. He put the box and shovel into the back of the vehicle and drove away slowly.

"I just saw her." Derek was pale and breathless. "Meg."

Connie was lifting a plate from the sink, and it remained in mid-air. "What are you talking about?"

"Where's Luke?"

"Out with the animals."

"Hang on."

Derek found the younger man looking over a sheep. "Come inside. I need to talk to you and Connie."

"Okay, won't be a minute."

"Quick."

When he had them both together, he began the story again, pausing halfway to recognise that he was sounding ridiculous.

"I know it sounds silly."

"Hey, we've had weirder things than that happen. You couldn't talk to her, hey?"

"She didn't see me."

"Hmm. Another thing to add to the bag of mysteries." Luke smiled.

Connie patted Derek's hand. "You're looking a bit pale."

"Yeah, well—it was like seeing a ghost."

They sat in silence, lost in their own thoughts.

"The journals. I have them now. Time to start

reading." Derek moved and winced. The digging had made his back even worse. "I'll see you at dinner time."

As he left the room, the young couple looked at each other with raised brows. Connie shrugged. "Perhaps we're all going a bit mad."

Luke laughed. "Speak for yourself!"

The first journal had a high-quality cover which appeared to be hand-stitched. Meg's writing wasn't a beautiful flowing script, but it was neat. She had evidently used a fountain pen.

The subsequent books were plainer, although still with high-quality paper. The entries in these more recent journals resembled a report rather than a window into Meg's mind. Derek could see they were going to be very useful nonetheless.

After quickly scanning some entries and sorting the books into date order, he settled on the window-seat and began reading. A cooling coffee sat on the floor beside him. Occasionally he would look out the window, diverted by a bird swooping onto the dam, and consider what he'd just learned.

Meg's experience of waking on the thirteenth of May, 2013 was as traumatic as his own. She had barely survived a childbirth that had claimed the life of the infant, only to find that, while she'd been unconscious, everybody else had died. This included her parents and two children by her ex-husband.

Like Derek, she went through various stages of grief and thoughts of suicide. She also got drunk, but only once, unlike Derek, who made drinking his new career for some time.

When the electricity supply to Melbourne stopped, she decided to move to Maleny, a decision prompted by a dream in which her ex-husband had stated, "This would be a good place to live when the world finally fucks up."

She took a four-wheel-drive from a motor dealer and drove north. On the way, she found lookouts, and stood at the top of each one, scanning the view for any sign of human life. There was none.

She searched for and found the house she'd been dreaming about. Constructed of rammed earth and totally self-sufficient for power and water, it was ideal.

Luke appeared suddenly one day, injured and mute. Meg cared for him and helped restore his health until one day he left on a motorbike without saying goodbye. Meg tracked him down and discovered he had to get to Cairns quickly, but she didn't know why. She drove him there, to a particular address. He ran inside the house and came out with a girl who was near death. They had arrived just in time to save her.

Through this girl, Connie, Meg discovered that Luke and the girl were strangers, brought together by vivid dreams. They felt like they already knew each other and quickly formed a bond.

Through another dream, Luke and Connie were instructed to 'become man and wife' which they did quite quickly. Soon Connie was pregnant with twins, which Meg helped bring into the world. There was a girl, Maisie, and a boy, Thomas. The boy failed to thrive.

Derek paused and rose to stretch his legs. He knew what was going to happen next and he needed a break before reading it. He made a fresh coffee and performed some yoga stretches to ease his back pain. Finally, he sat down again and found his place.

On the 30th November 2014, Derek and three other men had arrived at the Maleny house. Derek had unwittingly led them there, a fact he later regretted. He had met them several days before and was initially excited to find other survivors. They were the first people he'd seen in more than eighteen months. They had asked where he was headed and he'd told them there was a house in Maleny he needed to get to. What he didn't tell them was that he was being led there by incredibly detailed dreams.

The three others, who he discovered were brothers, said they'd walk with him. Initially this seemed like a good idea, and he was grateful for the company. As time went by, however, their immature and drunken behaviour began to annoy him. They all had base personalities and were poorly educated.

When they arrived at the house, the three brothers suggested they watch the place first to see what the story was. They were excited to find two females there, along with a supply of fresh food. After learning all there was to know, two of them, Derek and Jeff, stayed at the rear of the house, while the other two brothers walked up the driveway.

Meg's journal picked up the story at that point. She'd seen the two brothers coming, alerted by the animals' erratic behaviour. She had taken the rifle from the shelf where it was kept in case of dog attacks, and met them at the front of the house. They menaced and threatened her. She could hear Connie screaming in the house and realised there were more men. When one of the brothers aimed his shotgun at her, Meg fired the rifle several times and killed him. The other brother went to shoot her, so she dispatched him as well. Then she went to Connie's rescue.

Derek stopped reading and closed his eyes, remembering Meg coming in behind him and shooting the third brother. She'd then aimed the rifle at Derek, hesitating when she saw he was holding Thomas. Now, recalling the scene, Derek laughed to himself. He'd had to do some fast talking to get Meg to lower the firearm, but they had ended up being friends. He was even able to help by treating Thomas' heart defect.

He'd stayed with Meg, Luke, Connie, and the children long enough to help build a fence surrounding the property, and to ensure that Thomas' condition was stabilised. He left quickly after that, leaving only a note behind. The ghosts from his past kept chasing him, ensuring that he couldn't settle and find happiness.

In Meg's journal he lived that time through her eyes and realised how hard it was for her to accept his leaving, given that she was the 'only girl in the world' as the old song went. She felt abandoned, although he'd never given her any reason to think he would eventually be with her.

Thinking of this made him relive the vision he saw earlier in the day, a different version of Meg at the library. He shivered. What was that about?

He realised the sun was setting over the dam. He was late for dinner at Luke and Connie's. The other journals would have to wait.

The scene that greeted Derek at the other house was a sort of controlled chaos. Noisy children ate food messily, the adults trying to hush them. Heather was sitting on the sofa with her feet on a box, holding her swollen belly. George seemed to be trying to placate her while also begging their children to behave.

As he walked in the door, Derek was aware of all the adults suddenly turning their eyes to him. A hush fell over the room.

"Hi everyone. How's it all going?"

Several voices began talking at once. Derek held up his hands. "One at a time. Yes John?"

"You took the four-wheel drive. We needed it to tow a caravan here."

Derek slapped his forehead. "Bugger. Sorry, John. First thing tomorrow. I got caught up with other things.

Luke walked in from outside. "Hey Derek. Went fishing today at Baroon Pocket. Caught twenty."

"Good man. Fish for dinner, then?"

"Yeah, Connie decided to feed the kids first and put them to bed so we can talk over dinner."

Derek nodded and then approached Luke, motioning to him to go outside.

"Any issues?"

"Yeah. A few. We need a leader."

"George, I reckon."

"Nah, you."

Derek shook his head. "Don't want the job."

"Please? Just until we get sorted. Then you can hand it over to George."

"Don't you think George is a good choice?"

"Maybe, maybe not."

"I don't see John as a leader. He seems to go around with his head in the clouds."

"India?"

"I don't know anything about her. Even when they were all living with me—she seemed remote and a bit," he paused while searching for the right word. "Emotionless."

"Could be a good thing in a leader. Anyway, she's not emotionless about John."

"No, when it comes to him she's almost over the top. It's a bit extreme."

"Perhaps there's just you then, as leader."

"Maybe. Okay—look. I'll think it over. Let's go back inside."

"We need a big barbecue. Big enough to feed everyone in one go. We'll have a look tomorrow."

Everyone nodded in agreement. Luke cleared his throat.

"I think we need a leader, at least in the short term. Someone to make decisions and sort us all out. I think it should be Derek. What does everybody else say?"

"Great idea." John was beaming. Others were nodding.

Derek stood and made a shushing gesture with his hands. "No, wait. I'm not sure—"

George stood and raised his glass of water. "To our new leader, Derek. Certainly the best man for the job."

There were noises of agreement. Derek frowned but then nodded. "Okay, if that's what everyone wants, but I insist it's only for the short term. Once things are moving smoothly I'd like to pass it on to someone else. We'll discuss that down the track."

Connie moved into the kitchen and returned with a pie. "The kids have had theirs. We'll divide this one between us. Um, we need plates and spoons." Luke moved to the kitchen to get them.

They ate the pie in silence. All that could be heard was the clinking of cutlery on china and the murmuring of appreciation. The children were making soft sounds in the other room. Heather sighed and rested a hand on her belly.

Derek put his spoon down. "I've decided that my main

job from now on is to discover what's going on—in the world. I want to find out what killed all the people. I want to find out what's going on now. I'll need your help."

Everyone nodded silently. Then John spoke up. "What can we do?"

"I know we've spoken about this before, guys." He looked at John and George. "But explain to the others how you came to be at my house in Noosaville—how you found me."

Both John and George looked embarrassed. John spoke first. "This is going to sound silly."

"I'm sure it won't."

"You tell them, George."

George looked uncomfortable. "John and I compared notes. We found we both had dreams." Connie gasped.

Derek leaned forward and looked at him closely. "Describe them."

"Really vivid—telling us to go there and find you. We were in a pretty bad way, and the voice in the dreams said we'd find help there."

"Okay. Believe it or not, you're not the only ones. Connie, Luke and I have had them as well. Earlier on." He paused. "What I need you all to do is write down everything you know. How things happened on May 13th. What has happened since? Any theories you might have, however outlandish. This whole thing means we have to think outside the square."

There was silence.

"I'd prefer if you don't discuss it among yourselves first. Okay?"

"Sure." That was George. "How about we do it tonight, folks?" There were murmurs of agreement.

"Oh, and while you're doing that, can you also give me a list of skills you have—however minor? It might be a hobby or talent or something. Tell me what you've done as jobs, even part-time while you were studying at school or university. All that sort of thing. Okay?"

"I'll get some paper and pens," said Connie as she hurried off.

After the meal was finished, the clean-up done, and the children settled down to sleep, silence fell over the living room as the seven adults scribbled on pads of paper. Some worked slowly, staring into space from time to time before resuming their writing, while others wrote furiously without pause.

Derek only pretended to write the same answers as the others. He didn't want to describe the morning he woke to find his wife and children dead. He didn't need to list his hobbies, interests and skills. Instead he took a few minutes to describe Meg's otherworldly appearance at the library while it was still fresh in his mind.

Slowly, one by one, the other adults finished writing and added their pages to the pile on the coffee table. India was last. Derek gathered the sheets together and smiled.

"Great work, everyone. I'll look at these tonight and come up with some suggestions for rosters. Okay?"

John leapt to his feet. "You're going now then, Derek?"

"Yes, why?"

"Because you're going to disappear with the big car again. We need the tow-bar"

"Ah, yes. Caught me. I'll take the small sedan." He stopped and thought. "These two cars are both still running. I guess it's because they've been used a lot. We should put some more effort into finding some more that still work."

Luke put his hand up. "I've been learning about servicing and repairing cars and tractors. I found some books at the library. I reckon I could help."

"Good one, mate. See you all tomorrow night."

That night, back at his house, Derek skipped forward in Meg's journals to near the end. He read her account of the helicopter crash, and her words clearly transmitted the distress she felt. She was ill and frightened. Having already been through three complicated labours, one resulting in the death of the child, she knew the danger she was in by trying to give birth to twins without expert medical intervention.

He admired the course of action she took next, calmly assessing the situation and deciding that she should induce the births immediately. She found some hormone gel in Nambour hospital, applied it quickly and went into labour that night. Sadly, she and the twins died.

But who was the father of these twins? Not he, despite what Luke said. That was impossible. Rather than read the journals in the proper order, Derek now found he had to solve this mystery. Working out that conception would have taken place mid-November 2015, he found the journal that covered that period and settled down to read.

Meg was on the roof checking the solar panels after the cyclone when she saw Derek lying at the bottom of the driveway, unconscious. Luke helped carry him to her bedroom, where they tried to warm and revive him with body heat, hot water bottles, and blankets. He remained cold and comatose.

He was in Meg's bed and she was beside him, trying to keep him warm through the night. She woke to discover

Derek aroused and trying to enter her, and she accommodated him. He quickly satisfied himself and resumed sleeping.

In the morning Meg saw him moving naked from the bedroom to the living room. His walk was clumsy and uncoordinated. He then disappeared despite the house being marooned by flood waters and the fact he was naked. That was the last she saw of him.

Derek stopped reading and shivered in the same way he did after witnessing Meg's appearance at the library.

Reading further he was shocked by Meg's sense of abandonment after he allegedly left her the second time. Poor woman. She'd had a rough time at the hands of her husband, and then later was further humiliated by her photographer boyfriend. She deserved better.

While staring into space, his hands slowly closed the journal. He was more determined than ever to solve these mysteries. Why did everybody die? Who impregnated Meg? How did Meg appear at the library? Who was in the helicopter?

Derek's mouth was set into a thin line. He just had to discover the truth.

CHAPTER THREE

Derek slowed for the corner, conscious of the corrugations in the road. Luke was clutching the passenger grab-handle with both hands as they took the turn. Both men's teeth chattered as the whole vehicle shook. Derek swore.

"I can see that one of us will have to learn to drive a grader and fix some of these roads."

Luke smiled. "I'd like that!"

"Yeah, I bet you would. Better than milking cows, eh?"

"You bet!"

"Time for breakfast. I'll cook you something."

They had been back to the crash site to secure the tarp more firmly. Derek felt certain there were clues to be gained from the bodies and cargo. As they approached Derek's house, he saw something that made him brake suddenly. "Hey, look!"

"Where?"

"Can't you see it?"

"What?"

"Damn. I hoped you would."

It was the red car again, still almost transparent and shimmering. Meg had pulled up to the side of the road and was watching the house that she used to live in.

"Oh, wait. Yeah, I see something. It's red."

"It's Meg again. I'm glad I'm not the only one who can see it. She's moving off now." Derek accelerated again and began following the sports car.

"Where are we going? I'm starving!"

Meg's car was taking the corners of the dirt road easily. It was as though the holes and corrugations didn't exist for her. Derek tried to keep up, but eventually Meg and the shimmering car disappeared into the distance.

Derek sighed and turned the vehicle around.

"Now you're making me feel weird. It must feel like she's haunting you."

"No mate, I know what that's like. Sophie, my wife — deceased wife—she haunted me for a long time. I thought it would never stop." He turned his head and looked out the passenger window. After a few moments he cleared his throat. "This thing with Meg, it isn't like that. It's like watching a movie. I'm seeing something that's happening, but it's not really happening right in front of me—even though it appears to be. Do you see?"

"Ah, yeah. Sort of."

"Anyway, let's forget about it now." He drove through his gates. "Breakfast it is."

Derek finished washing the dishes and raised an eyebrow at Luke. "Your turn to wipe up, mate."

"Yeah, listen to this for a minute. I'm looking through the info you got the other guys to write down. You know, their interests and jobs and stuff?"

"Oh yeah. I fell asleep reading Meg's journals last night —didn't get to those sheets. Hey, you'll be interested to know that I read her account of when I came back after the cyclone."

"That must've been really interesting for you."

"Yeah. Weird. I'll get to the bottom of this yet."

"Anyway, so you haven't seen India's sheet?"

"Nup. Not yet."

"She used to run the Genomics lab at the University of Queensland."

"Get outta here."

"No, really. It's all here."

"So she's a geneticist?"

"Dunno. Some sort of scientist."

Derek whistled. "What are her hobbies?"

"She's a real geek. Mathematics for a hobby? Computer games."

"A super-brain. That could come in really handy."

"Yeah, fancy having someone like her cleaning our toilets."

"But what can she do now? No equipment, but it gives me food for thought."

Luke noticed that Derek had dried the dishes during that conversation. He smiled and turned to the next page.

CHAPTER FOUR

Derek cleared his throat. "Okay, everyone. I reckon you'd all be fairly happy with how things are going now? We've achieved a lot in the past couple of weeks. Everybody is comfortable, and we have all the facilities we need. We have plans to extend the solar power panel system as well as the turbines." There was nodding all around.

"The farm is producing enough food for everyone, and you all know your jobs. As far as I know everyone is doing what they're meant to. Are there any problems?"

"No, mate. It's bloody fantastic. You know, I never thought we could live like this." George waved his arms around the room. "I thought I'd landed in hell a few years ago. I thought I'd die alone somewhere, sick and sad. Now I've got Heather and a beautiful new family and a great place to live." There was scattered applause.

"Thanks, George. Yes, we're lucky, all right."

"Shame we haven't got a woman for you, fearless leader."

Derek's mouth twisted. "I don't think about that much, but this new world is full of surprises. You just never know what might happen next."

"We'll keep our eyes peeled for you."

"Thanks, mate. Anyway, now we have things working well here, I want to concentrate on my project. As you all know, I'm committed to finding out what happened in 2013. I also want to know more about some of the stranger aspects of this world we're living in."

He noticed India nodding with a look of rapt attention.

"We have few clues. There's a hospital out in the desert somewhere that I want to find. There are burned remains of three individuals to be examined. I'm going to call on all of you at different times to lend me some of your expertise."

"In what way?" Heather was frowning.

"Well, I've looked through those pages of information you gave me and was really surprised at the skills you all possess. Between us we have quite a depth of knowledge and experience. Take India here, for instance—amazing scientific and mathematical skills. John has studied ecology and sustainability, which I plan to put to use here. George has building skills. Heather is a school teacher." Derek stopped when he noticed Luke and Connie standing together, looking downcast.

"And take these two—Luke and Connie. They were too young to have acquired advanced learning or skills, but their knowledge of how things work around here is amazing. They are the backbone of this whole operation." Both the young people beamed.

"This is what I plan to do. I want to borrow India for a few days to help me with some testing of the crash victims. Is that okay with everyone? Can you all pitch in to help with what she does each day?" Heather and Connie both nodded.

"Next week I'm going to try and find the hospital. From my time there I remember that it wasn't new—wasn't built since everyone died. Would you agree, Luke and Connie?"

"Yeah, I reckon it was ten or fifteen years old." Luke looked at Connie for confirmation, and she nodded.

"Thanks, Luke. So it should be marked somewhere on a map and we have some clues to where it is from Meg's description of the flight."

"But you went there yourself."

"I know, John, but I was unconscious for both the trips there and back. Anyway, I'm going to need someone to come with me next week to help find it. You, John, have some orienteering experience. I reckon I could use you. Okay?"

"Yeah! Wow. Thanks, Derek."

"That'll give you a week to work out what we'll need. Make sure we have a good medical kit, compass, maps, ropes, and all that sort of stuff. Can you also check the four-wheel-drive out? Tyres and things."

Luke raised his hand. "I can do an oil change and check it over."

"Perfect. I'm amazed at what a talented group of people we have here!"

India raised her hand slowly. "That old PC in Luke and Connie's room. I'd like to check it out in case it's usable for my work on those bodies."

"Sure, but I reckon we can get you a better one at Maroochydore. There are some big electrical stores there, and we'll find you a couple of up-to-date ones—or the best there was in 2013 at least. Some monitors as well."

India smiled and nodded.

"In fact, make up a list of what you need. What scientific equipment would be useful? We can go and raid laboratories or places that supply them. It's a shame they don't have electricity or you could work in a proper lab."

"Yeah, that would have been something—being back in a lab again." India's tone was wistful.

An indignant howl came from the room where all the

children were.

"Give it back. Give it back. It's mine!"

Heather rolled her eyes and rose to break up the disturbance.

"That's about all for now, anyway. I'll pick you up at around ten in the morning, India, and we'll go and get you some gear."

India looked the happiest that Derek had seen her in the weeks since she and John had knocked on his door in Noosaville. She skipped from bench to bench, filling a large brown carton with a range of equipment. Occasionally she referred to a list that was broken into categories. One side featured safety items like gloves, goggles and lab-coat, while on the other side there were test tubes, petri dishes, and a large range of other items.

Derek bent over one of the desktop computers. "Maybe we should take one of these as well."

"Yeah, I thought so. Could have some good programs pre-loaded."

She opened another cupboard and sighed. "All this great gear. I never thought I'd see it again." More items were added to the box.

"Where did you and John meet?"

India brushed some hair from her forehead. "Um, it was around a year and a half since—you know—May 13th. I hadn't moved far from where I had been living in Brisbane. I wasn't doing really well and everything was such a struggle."

"Yeah, I know."

"I tried to be a bit philosophical, I guess you'd call it. But it didn't work. I was struggling to come to terms with everything. I'm a modern girl who likes modern stuff. I love technology. People had told me I loved it too much."

"So you wouldn't have been happy when electricity and the internet went away."

India closed her eyes. "It was just so bad I can't describe how I felt."

"So, then what happened?"

"It was a cool morning in Brisbane. Early spring. I was cold and went outside to sit in the sunshine. John came walking down the road!" She laughed. "I couldn't believe it! He was the first live person I'd seen in all that time."

"What did you do?"

"I think I rubbed my eyes or something silly like that. Perhaps blinked a few times. Then he caught sight of me and came running towards me. He stopped when he got about a metre away. Then we just looked at each other. For a long time. I think we'd both forgotten how to talk."

Derek saw the gleam of fondness in her eyes. She must've liked John from the outset.

"I think I moved first—moved until I was right under his nose."

"And then what?"

"Then he said something inane like, "What's a lovely thing like you doing in a place like this?" She laughed. "That broke the ice. We talked for ages—days. Then we sorta just stayed together."

"Then you got pregnant with twins."

"Yeah. Straight away."

"You didn't have children before?"

"No. These were my first. God it was hard! Poor John had to deliver them. We used contraception after that."

Derek nodded.

"I mean, look at poor, bloody Heather. Already advanced with her second set of twins. And Connie—so young to have four children already. That's just not me."

"I see your point. What does John think about all of this?"

"Oh, he'd have more. Feels a responsibility to re-populate the planet. Ha!"

"Hmm. Maybe down the track a bit."

"Maybe, but I'm not as young as Connie. I guess if we

were going to have more, it would have to be soon." She picked up another brown box and opened the four flaps. "Before, when I had my career, I didn't give motherhood a thought, you know? Felt it just wasn't for me."

"What do you think of it now?"

"I think John makes a great parent. I'm not sure about myself. I think I'll be better when they get older."

"Their health has improved dramatically since coming to Maleny."

"Yeah. Connie's so good with the cooking and she really loves to feed the kids, you know? Gets a kick out of seeing them enjoy the food. Amazing." She shook her head.

"I've noticed that you like to show children the wonders of nature—all the kids, not just yours."

"They're just sponges for knowledge at that age. Their eyes light up when I show them something miraculous. They could sit and watch a spider weave its web for ages if you tell them how it's producing the filament and how it weaves the pattern."

India's face was soft and lit with pleasure. Derek had never seen her so attractive.

"Perhaps as all the children get older, you can do a formal class once or twice a week. Biology or something."

"Yeah, wow. That would be great."

The second box was filling with larger items. She placed some books on top.

"Finished?" Derek hadn't wanted to rush her, but they'd been there a long time.

"Yeah. This is exciting. I can't wait to get back and set up."

She took one last look around the laboratory and then smiled at Derek. "Let's go."

Derek woke with a start. His body was lathered in sweat, and he could feel the damp sheet next to his skin.

Sophie. She had visited him again—she and the two children.

What had brought it on this time? Their visits had been lessening with the passing of time, and now there was always a reason, a trigger. He remembered how bad it had been when he first stayed with Meg, Luke, and Connie—so bad he had left and found somewhere else to live. He thought it had all calmed down enough for him to return to Maleny.

Now the haunting was back.

It was different each time, but there were common elements. This time they were on holiday, the four of them, in a unit at the beach. Derek and Sophie were inside, drinking a fruity cocktail with ice and watching the children play at the edge of the water.

Sophie was telling him an interesting story about her work as a paediatric anaesthetist—a procedure that went wrong—and he'd become engrossed in what she was saying. Sophie's well-bred British accent was always a joy to listen to, and when it also involved a subject he was interested in, he could get lost in her words. When he next looked around at the beach, one of the children was missing.

He stood suddenly, his drink smashing on the tiled floor. He could see a head bobbing in the water, twenty or so metres out. He tried to run across the sand, but couldn't make any progress. He was yelling and waving to his son.

The scene changed.

He and Sophie were bobbing in the ocean. She was laughing and the drops of sea water were sparkling on her eyelashes. She closed the gap between them and kissed him fully on the mouth. They were floating up and down with the movement of the waves, and he could feel her breasts pushing against his chest.

Sophie reached down until her hand slid into his board-shorts. He groaned.

The scene changed again.

Sophie was in the green cocktail dress, his favourite outfit of hers. He, himself, was wearing a dinner suit. They were standing in a crowded room, ornate like a ballroom, and there was music and laughter.

But Sophie was in tears. She was trying to tell him something, but he couldn't hear. She was gulping and hiccoughing, and he couldn't make out the words. The tears fell in droplets, staining the satin of her frock. "Tell me! What's the problem?" It didn't matter how much he tried to make out her words, they eluded him.

They were on the old sofa in the back room of the house in Coogee. It was morning and they both had coffee. Newspapers were spread over the furniture and the floor, and they were passing sections to each other and commenting on stories.

Sophie stood and yawned, stretching her arms high above her head. She grinned and leapt onto him, causing him a moment of panic so that he raised his knees to protect himself. She laughed and landed with her hands on the arm of the sofa behind him. She kissed him and nuzzled his neck. He lowered his knees so she could lay fully down the length of his body.

Their arousal was sudden and urgent. She straddled him and opened her robe so he could view her body. He licked his fingers and pushed them into her, checking her wetness. She was impatient and guided him into her with a gasp.

That's when he'd woken up.

Why? Why had the dreams come back?

Then he thought about the laboratory, about India and how he'd realised she was attractive. That explained it.

He moved the other side of the bed and tried to return to sleep, but his mind was now full of Sophie—the amazing, wonderful woman who had been his best friend, lover, wife, and mother to his children. Calm, rational, and non-judgemental, she'd been a dream to live with. She accepted everything and everyone at face value. She was adored by almost every person she ever met. Men and women were drawn to her equally.

Despite the fact she had a career, children, and a household to run, she always found time for him. Always. He never felt left out. She juggled all these aspects of her life without complaint, although sometimes he saw the fatigue shadowing her face.

She was also the only person who knew his greatest flaws. She knew them, understood them, and protected him from them. They were his sensitivity and lack of confidence, which he'd learned to hide behind a calm, professional facade. Only she knew how he crumbled when he had to give bad news to the worried parents of his child patients. It made him physically ill. He would arrive home shaking and retching, and she would always come to him. She would sit and hold his hand while he recounted the ordeal, squeezing his eyes in pain. He would always find a way to blame himself for the child's illness, always questioning his own ability. Could he have recognised the problem earlier? Treated the child in a different way? Many times he had decided to leave his career —considered himself wrong for it. The only thing that made his job bearable was knowing that Sophie would be there to patch him up again when he fell apart.

His lack of confidence wasn't confined to his work, but it also affected his everyday life. He always admired and was mildly jealous of men who walked through the world easily, exuding charm and confidence. Derek tried to emulate them, find his own easy grace, but he could never quite carry it off.

Once, in late summer, they went for a holiday to New Zealand with another couple and their children. They stayed at a wilderness lodge on Marlborough Sound, enjoying the unspoiled beauty of the region.

One morning they all went hiking and returned to the lodge for lunch. They found an idyllic place to rest and relax, sitting on chairs that had been placed on the lawn under huge, spreading umbrellas. There were groans of pleasure as they eased sore muscles. The menu was discussed and orders were placed.

Derek became aware of a reflection in the broad windows of the dining room. There was a man, tall, lean and good-looking. He was well-groomed and, although dressed in casual clothing, carried the look of success.

He was sitting among a number of people and the dynamics of this group were such that this man was listened to with interest and also had his opinion sought regularly.

The children in the group were very comfortable around him, using his body as a playground—placing their trusting arms around his neck and giving him kisses.

Derek watched this man, this confident and charismatic man, with fascination, until the light changed and the reflection disappeared. He was disappointed to have lost that vision, that wonderful representation of himself, which was of a man he liked and admired.

Now, without Sophie, he was simply empty. When she died, everything good in him was sucked out. All that remained was his lack of confidence and over-sensitivity. It was all too hard. Thinking about her now, the loss of her, made him groan out loud.

Knowing it was useless to lie there further, awake and fretting, he rolled out of bed. There were always Meg's journals to read.

The sun was rising over the Glasshouse Mountains when Derek finally closed the journal and looked at his notes. He'd been fascinated with the story of how Meg had scored a top position, Executive Assistant to Angela Morris, on the basis of the results of a psychometric profile test. She had found, to her amazement, that she was perfect for the role.

He'd had some experience with these tests, had even had to take one once, but had never heard of them being used in such a definitive manner.

Meg's account of how she'd been ruthlessly dumped by two men in her life, her husband Richard and then a fashion photographer, had angered him. Although she'd written about these events simply and without too much emotion, her pain had been clear.

The sad part was she saw him, Derek, as another who had abandoned her. In the aftermath of the cyclone, when the Derek impostor had come and impregnated her and then left without a word the next morning, Meg had once again pondered why the men in her life treated her in that way.

Derek doodled as he considered how this must have hurt her. He found himself feeling her pain and pulled back. There was no use dwelling on that now. Besides, he had an appointment with India, who was going to discuss her findings on the three bodies from the helicopter.

"This is the most interesting thing." India poked a piece of skull with a pencil end. "The skull is different to normal. It's sort of elongated and widens near the top."

Derek frowned. "So, what are you saying? Was it human?"

"I'll be able to say for sure after running tests later, but I'm fairly certain it is. Just, I don't know, like it's been modified."

"An upgraded human?"

She laughed. "Perhaps more advanced is the right terminology."

Derek whistled. "More advanced. Wow."

"But I really don't know anything yet. That's just an educated guess."

"What about the other two""

She walked to the next table, fanning herself with a sheath of paper. "We could do with air-conditioning in here." She took the covering from the second figure. "This one shows no abnormalities, seems like a normal human."

"Okay. Did he have a chipped tooth?"

"One of them did, but I'm not sure which. Some teeth had come loose from the skull."

"So it belonged to number two or three. What can you tell about the third one?"

"Very similar to number two. Strangely similar."

"Twins?"

"Could be and I can run those tests later. For now, number one is my main priority."

"Hmm. I can see why. Must be interesting."

"You could say that. Hey, I might need to go to Queensland University to use some of their equipment."

"The lab you used to work in?"

"Yeah. I need to run some very advanced tests."

"What about the lack of power?"

"No probs. There's a backup generator there. I'd need a few days."

"I can't see a problem with that. John and the girls can look after Marie and Peter."

"Great. I'll leave the day after tomorrow."

"What about food and things? You'd better take some with you."

"Yeah, I can sort that. Don't worry. I never eat much when I'm working on a big project." She pushed her glasses back up her nose. "I wish some of my colleagues were here to see this." She pointed to the first figure.

"To run ideas past them?"

"No, just to show them. No one has ever seen anything like this before."

"Really?"

"Oh, yeah! This is quite extraordinary."

CHAPTER FIVE

Derek turned his face towards the warmth of the mid-morning sun and closed his eyes. He was sitting on the small pier-like structure that jutted over the dam. The wood was worn and weathered and seemed older than the house. Not for the first time, Derek wondered why the structure was originally built, then came to the conclusion that maybe it was for that exact purpose—a pleasant place to sit and drink coffee in the morning.

It would be a good place for meditating, if you were so inclined, he thought, which he wasn't. He remembered Sophie's struggle with trying to still her mind—going so far as buying special cushions and placing a small altar in the corner of a room, which contained candles and flowers and a statue of Buddha. Nothing worked, however. Her brain was always too busy.

"I'm sure it's not meant to be this difficult". She would be frowning after these sessions, and Derek would suggest that she might be trying too hard.

"You're so many things to so many people that your mind is never still."

"I know that! That's why I'm trying to meditate!"

Derek smiled sadly at the recollection. He took a sip of coffee and leaned back in the chair. One of the journals lay unopened on his lap. He closed his eyes and listened to the world.

A rustling in the bushes interrupted this activity. He opened his eyes and was greeted with the sight of a snake moving across the grass toward the pier. Another followed. Both were short and muscular looking. Derek had no fear of snakes and watched them almost idly, without concern.

When a third and fourth viper came towards the pier, Derek decided to move into the house and close the door. He didn't feel like trying to evict snakes from his home.

Once inside, he looked at the journals yet to be read and decided he wasn't in the mood. John and India's son, Peter, had been suffering a chest infection and should be checked. Derek left through the front door, closing it tightly.

As he backed out of the driveway, he saw more snakes—or were they the same ones? They appeared to be trying to head in his direction across the stones that made up the driveway. He shook his head at this strange sight and kept driving.

Nobody appeared to be outside at the community house, which was unusual. He parked the car at the front door and saw Luke appear at the window next to it. He was waving and indicating that Derek should stop and stay where he was.

Connie appeared beside Luke and they spoke urgently for a few moments. Derek drummed his hands on the steering wheel. He heard a scream——a man's scream of pain. Luke and Connie looked at each other and Connie moved off swiftly, re-appearing with a piece of paper and black marker.

Luke wrote in block capitals: WATCH OUT FOR SNAKES. WE'LL GET YOU INSIDE.

Derek opened the car door and saw at least ten adders start to move toward him, and their movement reminded him of iron filings being drawn to a magnet. He closed the door quickly and waited for Luke to finish writing the next instalment: DRIVE RIGHT UP TO THE DOOR. GET ON THE CAR BONNET. I'LL OPEN THE DOOR AND U JUMP IN.

There was nothing in that message that Derek was happy with, but he knew Luke to be sensible. There had to be a good reason. He moved the car closer to the front door of the house and opened the car door. He manoeuvred himself onto the door runner and then over onto the bonnet. A bolt of pain shot through his lower spine, causing him to swear.

He balanced himself on the bonnet. Luke gave him the thumbs-up and showed him the rake he was holding. The front door opened and Luke positioned himself with the rake on the ground at the ready.

"Jump!" Now!"

Derek leapt across the small distance and into the house. When he turned to speak to Luke, he saw him beating a snake that was caught halfway across the door frame, preventing the door from closing properly. Connie came with a broom and they managed to push the partially squashed creature outside before slamming the door closed. Connie arranged rolled-up towels along the bottom of the entry.

A man's scream had Luke and Connie running past Derek, who was momentarily frozen by the sound. When he went to move, his back spasmed. He felt like screaming as well, but walked slowly toward the source of the terrible noise.

"Please, John. Please just let us—" Heather's pleas were drowned out by John's screams.

George was trying to hold the man down with minimal success. He raised his head when Derek entered. "Gee, mate—great to see you. Know much about snake bite?"

"I didn't think Australian snakes caused this kind of pain."

"I didn't think Australian snakes glided out of trees, either, but it's happening. There are two sorts..."

"Which one bit John?"

"Two of the short ones."

John sat upright with a suddenness that almost caused George to topple backwards. Then he went stiff and fell back on to the tiled floor with a sound like an egg smashing. He went very still.

Derek crossed over to where John was lying. He picked up a wrist and felt it. Then he felt a spot in the man's neck. Next he got down on all fours and placed his ear on John's chest. "Gone."

Silence fell over the house, even from the room where Connie was keeping the children. The adults looked at each other, and Heather whispered, "Poor John. What a way to die." She sat heavily in a dining chair and began sobbing silently.

Derek became aware of a rustling above his head. He looked at the ceiling and saw George do the same thing. Heather's sobs turned to whimpers. "God, they're in the roof!" Her eyes were round and unblinking.

George began walking around the room, his eyes

swivelling around the ceiling. He ran into the next room, then the next. "Okay everyone. We have to plug these vents. Grab a chair and some rags or towels or something. Quickly!"

Five adults swung into action and plugged any gaps where the snakes might access the living areas. "Thank God this is a solid rammed-earth house." George was breathing heavily from exertion. "No wall cavities. Otherwise our friends up there might have got closer to us." He stood in the middle of the lounge area, the stained glass windows colouring his pale face. "We have to make sure the kiddies don't open doors or windows under any circumstances."

"Perhaps we should keep them in that bedroom for the time being. It's crowded, but at least we can keep track of them."

"Good idea. Hey, Connie. Did you hear what Derek just suggested?"

"Yes, Heather and I will keep them in here."

The rustling from the roof cavity was getting on Derek's nerves. "It feels almost biblical, you know?"

George nodded. "Yeah, mate. I know what you mean. Where in the hell could so many snakes come from?"

"Not only that—they seem to really be trying to get at us. It's just not normal."

"Yeah, and they did get one of us. Poor bloody John."

Derek frowned. "Hey, where's India?"

"Out in that laboratory of hers. We yelled out to her to stay there and not open the door until we come and get her."

"So she doesn't know about John?"

George shook his head slowly.

Derek moved to the windows and looked out towards the shed where India was trapped. The expanse between the two buildings was writhing with adders.

"How did they get John?"

"He was out at the four-wheel-drive, getting stuff ready for your trip. The snakes were on us before we knew much about what was happening—the kids were playing around the chook house. John yelled at them to get inside, but they didn't move at first. Didn't understand what was going on. He ran and picked up two of the young ones, one under each arm, and then began running inside while yelling at the older ones to follow. Then he went back for more. He got bitten twice, but saved all the kids."

"Brave man."

"You know—without him, a lot of the kiddies would have got bitten."

"Thank God he saw the snakes when he did."

Derek turned his thoughts to India out in the shed they'd converted to a laboratory. It wasn't as well sealed as the house. What was she going through out there on her own? His first instinct was to rescue her somehow, but he quickly realised that would be impossible.

Hopefully the snake attack would stop soon.

It was another day before they realised the rustling in the roof cavity had stopped. Connie ran to the big window in the living room and looked over the property. "They're all dead!" Heather ran to her side and they stood, transfixed by the sight of so many dead snakes.

"My God."

Derek heard what the women were saying and called for George and Luke. The five adults stood at the windows watching for any sign of movement across the grass. Derek pointed. "They all look dead but we'll have to make absolutely bloody certain of it before we go out."

"Poor India." Connie's eyes were filling with tears. "We should try to get her as soon as we can."

The noise from the bedroom where the children were confined was rising. Heather sighed. "They're getting cabin fever. Do you think it's okay to let them loose in the house now?"

Derek frowned. "Okay, but keep a close eye on them, just in case."

Heather walked toward the bedroom calling to the children. Luke and Connie followed. Derek pulled two chairs to the windows. "Let's sit and watch for half an hour. If we don't see anything move, I'll go for India."

Derek was wrapping towels around his legs before pulling the denim from his jeans legs down over them. He then wrapped scarves over those. Long boots were pulled on next.

Luke frowned. "What about the ones that glide down from the trees?"

"Good point, mate. I'll take that broad-brimmed hat. At least with those ones I'll be able to see them coming."

"Here's another scarf". Connie came out of their bedroom and wrapped it around his neck. "Just in case. We don't want to lose you as well."

"Okay, well——I'm as ready as I'll ever be."

George slid the glass door open just enough for Derek to slip though. "The rake is just to the right, there." Derek nodded and reached for the tool as the door closed behind him.

Not wanting to stand on the dead adders, he pushed them aside with the rake to create a clear path. When he got to the shed door, he stopped and listened. No sound. He took a deep breath and steeled himself for whatever he might find.

The door was hard to push open and Derek realised it was blocked by towels. He poked his head around the corner and saw India at a long bench, peering into a petri dish.

"Oh hello, Derek." She typed something into the computer.

"So, you're okay then?"

"Yes, fine."

"You must be hungry."

"Um...yeah, now that you mention it. I've been so absorbed in this" She waved her hand across the bench-top. "Number one over there has some very interesting qualities in his blood."

"Well, stop now. Come over to the house." He cleared his throat. "I'm afraid we have some bad news for you."

"Oh? What?"

"John."

India swivelled around on her stool. "What? What's wrong with him?"

"He was saving the children from the snakes—"

"No! No! Oh my God. Not John."

She stood then, but swayed and had to steady herself. Derek crossed to her quickly and held her by the shoulders. "Steady on."

"Not John. Jeez. He was the only man..." She began crying then—big sobs with hiccoughs at the end.

"There, there. Listen, I'll take you back to the house. They're all worried about you." He was hoping that Connie and Heather would have the right words to console her.

He supported her on the walk back to the house, moving slowly in time with her steps. George was waiting and pulled the door open. Connie ran up and enfolded India in an embrace.

"Where is he? I want to see him!"

Derek and George looked at each other. They hadn't thought of that.

"We put him in the laundry—the coolest room. He's all wrapped up ready for burial." Derek hardly finished the sentence before India ran off to the other side of the house. He followed quickly.

"You don't really want to see him, India. He was in a lot of pain. It shows. You're better off remembering him the way he was. He's also starting to smell."

She entered the laundry and stopped when she saw the wrapped figure on the floor. Her shoulders sagged, and she began swaying again. Derek moved quickly to support her.

"He was cute, you know. I guess not many would think so—I mean he was so pale and slight. He was balding, too, but in a nice way. When he took his glasses off, he was sort of handsome, you know?"

She removed her own glasses and rubbed the lenses with a cloth from the pocket of her lab coat.

"I've never had much to do with men or romance or anything. When John came walking along the road that day when I'd been so lonely and scared by myself—well, he just swept me off my feet."

She sat on the cool tiles and laid her hand on John's chest. "When will you bury him?"

"As soon as we're sure all the snakes are dead."

"When do you reckon that'll be?"

"Not sure. Perhaps tomorrow."

"Okay. Just leave me with him, will you?"

"Sure, but we haven't told your two kids. We thought you might want..."

"Yes. Send them in."

Derek stood for a moment, watching her attempts to pull herself together. Shoulders were straightened and hair was swept back from the face. "Hold on a minute". She went into the lounge and came back with three cushions which she placed near the body. "Okay."

Connie walked into the bedroom. When she came out a moment later, she was holding the hands of Peter and Marie whom she led to India. The laundry door closed.

Derek felt the dreaded aftermath coming, the shaking and retching caused by having to break the news to India. He excused himself and ran out the sliding door, trying desperately to find a private place to pull himself together. Sliding on carcasses of snakes, he made his way to India's laboratory and went straight through to the bathroom at the back. He was still wrapped in the towels and scarves he had worn as protection from snake bite. Angrily he tore at them and then at all his clothing, finally sinking to the bathroom floor where he sat naked and cried and shook and retched and howled for Sophie until he was so exhausted that he began to calm down.

CHAPTER SIX

Derek raised his glass. "To John".

"To John." The five adults lifted their drinks in a salute.

India's face was pale and tear-streaked. "Now that's over, I think it's time I went to UQ to run those tests."

Derek nodded. "And I have to drive out west and look for that hospital." He looked around him. "I guess we need to do this one at a time."

"Who are you going to take with you now?" George's face was hopeful.

"Nobody, damn it. I didn't really want to go alone, but I can't see I have any choice now. You're all needed here."

"Well, I don't think you should go alone. It's too dangerous. We couldn't do without you." Connie folded her arms. "I don't know what you expect to find there, anyway."

"Nor do I, but I'm less accepting of things than you. I've got to know what's going on."

Derek looked around all the faces. Heather was siding

with Connie. George was on his side. India was neutral. Luke swayed between the two camps.

Heather patted her swollen belly. "And don't forget these two. You'll need to be here for the birth."

"How many weeks are you now?"

She looked at George who shrugged. "Oh, probably thirty-seven or so."

"I tell you what. India can go to UQ first and investigate the bodies. Whether I go out west or not will be based on her findings."

There was general nodding.

"I'll go first thing in the morning." India said this with a clenched jaw.

"Sure. Make sure you take food and water with you. You can drive the pink hatchback. Have you checked it over thoroughly, Luke?"

Luke nodded. They had been able to retrieve two more vehicles from motor dealers, thanks to Luke's newfound mechanical knowledge.

India rose. "Okay. I'm going to the lab now to make a list of things to take."

Derek watched her walk out toward the smaller shed. She had been remote since John's death and seemed to have shrunken. "I'm worried about India. She's not doing well."

"I would be devastated if I lost George." Heather smiled at her man. "It was such a shock for her. I'm more worried about Marie and Peter. India hasn't really had anything to do with them since John died."

"They're so young they don't really know what's going on, but I know what you mean. Let's see if the time she spends away at UQ helps her." Derek was doubtful—India had never had a lot time for her children.

"I just realised something." Heather's face broke into a smile. "Marie and Peter. The names."

"What about them?"

"Marie Curie and her husband Pierre—you know—they discovered radium. I reckon they're named after them!"

George frowned and Luke and Connie looked puzzled. Derek was the only one that smiled. "Yes, you're probably right."

"C'mon Heather. You're nearly there. One last push."

Derek had his sleeves rolled up and was standing with his knees bent, reaching for the second twin. Heather grimaced and pulled against George's grip. She let out a hoarse cry as the tiny figure moved into Derek's hands.

"We should have known it would be two girls. Good girl, Heather. You did well."

Heather's smile was weak. "Thanks. It was easier this time with your help."

George feigned offence. "What? I wasn't a good enough midwife for you?" He was already holding the first-born twin and rocking her.

"I reckon you were close to fainting most of the time. It was better having you as a hand-holder."

Derek laid the girl on Heather's chest and pulled the blankets up around the two of them. "They both look fine, although this one is smaller. I'm sure she'll catch up."

Connie came to the door and smiled. "More of us. How wonderful. Cup of tea, Heather?"

"Love one, thanks."

Derek began tidying the mess caused by the birth. "Now that's over, I should really go and check on India."

"What, now? Can't you wait a day to make sure these two are okay?"

"I didn't mean right now, Heather. Probably tomorrow. I'm a bit worried about her."

"How long's it been?"

"Over a week. We need carrier pigeons or something. It's frustrating without communications."

"Do you want me to go?" George was smiling down at his new daughter.

"I think you've got enough on your hands. No, I reckon it'll have to be me."

Heather smiled. "You always seem to be going to India's rescue. I hope she appreciates it."

"I'm sure she doesn't notice."

"Both of you are single now—"

Derek looked at her sharply. "So?"

"Nothing. I was just saying—"

"It's the hormones," said George. "Take no notice, mate."

"Hmm. Anyway, I'll be at my house until one o'clock tomorrow afternoon if you need me. Then I'll head off to UQ and be back by nightfall."

Connie bustled in with a mug of tea. "Here we are, you brave thing. You did better than me. I was a mess."

"I'm sure you were very brave."

"Meg helped me a lot. I don't know what would've happened if she hadn't been there."

"Shame I never got to meet her."

"She was great, wasn't she Derek?"

"Wonderful woman. Hey, speaking of Meg, she always kept records of births. She asked you to keep the journals going."

He saw a look of confusion cross the young woman's

face.

"Oh, yes. Well—it's been kinda busy."

"I think Meg was right—we need to keep track of these things. Are you far behind?"

Connie nodded.

"Think you can catch up?"

"Yes, um, I think so."

"We should also make note of the snake attack. These things might be important in the future."

"Sure. I'll look at it tonight."

"Okay, I'm off. See you all tomorrow night."

As Derek gritted his teeth as he drove through the corrugations in the road, he realised he'd been hard on Heather. She'd touched a nerve in him, and he wondered about that.

Yes, he felt protective towards India. Yes, she was attractive in a geeky-girl sort of way. His original assessment of her gave way to admiration when he realised the extent of her intelligence and knowledge. She just wasn't made for group activities, or, indeed, playing mother. She had been crazy about John, but little else.

And he was sure that Heather just thought it would be nice to have another couple in the community, instead of two couples and two single people. It made sense.

The realisation came to him that it was going to be difficult in the future. He and India would be watched for signs of affection or attraction. There would be speculation. The very thought of it made him tired.

India had already said she didn't want more children. What was the point then? Maybe she would change her mind, though, and then expect him to be enthusiastic about the idea.

He sighed and slid into another patch of corrugations. A drive into the desert alone was starting to sound like a wonderful idea.

CHAPTER SEVEN

The Genomics and Computational Biology facility was one building in a sprawling campus that was the University of Queensland. This was an attractive seat of learning, with extensive sports grounds, water features and sandstone buildings.

As Derek drove further into the complex, he discovered a confusing series of small streets and angled buildings. He found a lake which boasted several species of bird life. The buildings beyond the lake seemed to belong to the Engineering department. He cursed and retraced his steps until he found the Genomics facility. He was relieved to see the fluorescent pink car in the parking area.

As he came to a stop he gazed at the building, wondering where to gain entry. The main doors looked heavily secured, and this was confirmed when he tried to open them. Moving around the side, he found a grey door that was being held open by a brick.

His eyes adjusted to the dim surrounds, and he listened

for clues to where India might be. The building was silent, however, and he found it necessary to search systematically, department to department.

India was on the second floor, in a room with glass walls which gave a fish-tank effect. At least he was able to spot her easily. She was seated with her head resting in the crook of her arm, which was flat on the bench.

He opened the door quietly and entered on the balls of his feet. As he crossed the room to her, he was relieved to see that she was breathing rhythmically.

He couldn't see any evidence of food and wondered where she ate and slept. He opened a few more doors close-by, but was none the wiser.

Returning to the room India inhabited, he looked around to see if he could judge her progress. There were notes written in a spiky hand with a black felt-tipped pen, but they may as well been Egyptian hieroglyphics for all the sense they made to him.

He looked at his watch and then strode to a window to check the sun's position. He cleared his throat. He then grabbed a chair and pulled it out from the table, making a screeching sound on the linoleum flooring.

India raised her head and looked around, finally focusing on Derek. "Oh, hey."

"Hey to you, too."

"I've found out some great stuff."

"Excellent. You can tell me all about it on the way back to Maleny."

"Huh?"

"It's time to go home."

"Really? How long have I been here?"

"Over a week, now."

"Oh, okay. Yeah, you want to drive out west."

"It's not only that. You're needed back there."

"Am I?"

"Peter and Marie—"

"Yeah. I guess so."

"Heather had her twins, too. Girls."

India gave a wan smile. "Great."

She stood and removed her lab coat, hanging it on a hook beside a cabinet. She was wearing a white t-shirt and low cut jeans underneath, and Derek could see her ribs and hip-bones clearly.

"It looks like you need some of Connie's home cooking, too."

India looked down at her body with disinterest. "I've been too busy."

"Let's pack up what you need."

India collected some empty boxes from an adjacent room and began piling objects into them.

"You can go. I won't be far behind you."

Derek shook his head. "We'll leave the pink terror here. If you need to come back, I'll drive you and you can return it after that."

"What if I don't need to come here anymore?"

"No big deal. It can stay here and we'll get another one from a motor dealer."

"Sure?"

"Yup. What can I pack up?"

"This is all I need. Let's go."

"C'mon. Tell me what you found."

"Well..." India pushed a strand of hair from her face and leaned against the door pillar of the four-wheel-drive. "What have we got—one and a bit hours 'till we get home?"

"Um, yeah. About that."

"So, I'm going to lead you to the conclusion, the same way I got there. Step by step."

"Okay."

"The great thing about our lab is that it has all the latest and best sequencing equipment. Between there and the genome research facility, I was able to do everything I wanted."

"So, power wasn't a problem, then?"

"Diesel generators. Still worked fine."

"So?"

"So, I sequenced number one's DNA."

"So far so good."

"Then I looked at the mitochondrial or mtDNA. It's a separate genome that all cells have—so it's a way to track and trace lineage and evolution."

"I see."

"Yeah, you see—mutations in the mtDNA are used as markers."

"So how did you do this? What equipment?"

"Well, to start with I had to break up the tissue sample by digesting it."

"Digesting it?"

"Yeah, I used digestive enzymes and detergent. Then I filtered it to get the lumps out. That's all I needed to do to create a sample."

"How long did all that take?"

"Only half a day or so, but before that I had to set everything up. By day two I was able to begin running the sequencing. Not long ago it used to take days for the sequencing to run. Now it's only around and hour and a half."

"Wow."

"So, for the sequencing I found a stack of nanopore sequencing chips and a couple of laptops to read the output. So I can finish the rest in Maleny on the portables."

"Really?"

"That's for the other two bodies, two and three. I've finished number one."

"Okay, so you sequenced number one's DNA. What did you find?"

"This is the fun part. I compared his DNA to a human reference sequence—the last one was HG20, which is version 20 of a composite human genome sequence. It's well assembled and heavily annotated. It was the one we were using in 2013 before..."

"Before everyone died."

"Yeah. So I compared the two sequences and the results were just mind-blowing."

"Tell me the highlights. In layman's terms please."

"I have been talking in layman's terms! So many mutations and I've never seen these and I can't find evidence that any other researcher has seen them before, either. It's so exciting!"

"What sort of mutations?"

"Before I tell you that, I need you to think ahead a few

hundred years. Think about what will be happening to humans in that time."

"Hard to tell. There are so few of us. Our diet is okay just now. We're doing more manual work than before May 2013."

"Good. What else?"

"Um, scientifically speaking? Wow. We have to think harder. Our brains were getting lazy before 2013—could just look up anything on the web. Now we need to use our long-term memory again. Think harder."

"Good. Keep going."

"How far into the future?"

"Oh, I'd say a few hundred years, maybe four or five."

"I reckon that we humans would get technology back on track fairly quickly—we'd find ways. Just imagine what your children could achieve with your genes and the right early education and ongoing learning."

"Yes, that's right."

"Four hundred years, say? Well let's think about what we have achieved in the past four hundred years—from 1616 onward. Wow. I'd have to think."

"Yeah, well I already did that—the UQ library made it easy. We started with King Charles I in England. The establishment of the East India Company. Shakespeare wrote

Hamlet. The first permanent English colony on the American mainland was established in Virginia. Scientifically, Galileo was looking at the moons of Jupiter through his telescope. John Napier discovered logarithms."

"Really?"

"Yup. Then the Ming Dynasty in China ended. We move into the next century. There was the invention of the steam engine, then the spinning machine and the industrial revolution began. Nitrogen was discovered."

"It all seems to accelerate after that."

"Indeed. In the 1800's we made passenger railroads, the first photograph was taken. Anaesthetic was used for the first time."

"Ether?"

"Yes. The wars are what made technology really surge forward and there were plenty of those, globally."

"So if we look at what we achieved in the past four hundred years and then try to use that as a basis for the next four hundred..."

"Yes, but everyone died except us. Technology is set back—well not set back but stalled. But as you say, I reckon we'll be quick to re-establish it."

"So what does all this mean in terms of genetic mutations?"

"I can see we did okay. This is what I found in number one's DNA." India opened a notebook. "Amplification of a number of neurotransmitter pathways—that means elevated processing speed. A depletion of genes associated with long-term memory, which means that the internet type technology gets going again quickly. Partially disabled immune system, suggesting readily available antimicrobial, antiviral, anticancer drugs, and prevention of allergies and autoimmune diseases."

"My God."

"It doesn't end there. There's evidence of amplified anabolic steroid production. This would be to build muscle mass without exercise in a sedentary lifestyle."

"So we go back to being couch potatoes."

India laughed. "Yeah. I guess so."

"The technology is still there—we haven't lost it. We just have to get it going again."

"And clearly we manage to do just that."

"That's nice to know."

"Don't forget we don't know what's going on in other countries. There could be cells of survivors like us."

"The northern hemisphere was such a mess. Meg looked on the webcams and saw it. It was late afternoon when everyone died, so there were crashes and fires and it looked like hell. Especially compared to here, where it happened around two in the morning."

"Hmm. I guess we were lucky in that way, if you can call it that."

"I'm struggling to get my head around what you've discovered. This man, person one from the helicopter crash, his DNA was really advanced. So what are you suggesting?"

"I'm suggesting he is from the future. That's what the best of scientific evidence suggests."

Derek fell silent. His brain was whirring at full speed. How can this be? How did this man travel back in time?

India began chatting again—talking about the testing and equipment and the science behind genome sequencing. As they turned into the Landsborough-Maleny Road, however, and began the steep climb up the range to the house, India's talk lessened. Derek could feel her withdrawal —sense the barriers rising.

He knew why this was happening—he'd been in this exact position many times. She was preparing herself for the hurt of John's absence. She would still half expect him to rush to greet her, to open his arms, to smile in his disarming way. Derek knew how much this would hurt.

Finally they turned into the driveway and began the steep climb to the house. Derek was pleased to see Peter and Marie playing outside, supervised by Heather. As she saw the vehicle approaching, Heather motioned to the two children and talked to them, nodding towards the car. They beamed and ran toward India, their plump little legs moving almost too fast for their bodies. Peter almost fell, but corrected himself.

"Mummy! Mummy!" they cried as India opened her door. Derek noticed the softening of her face as she climbed out of the car to greet her children.

CHAPTER EIGHT

Derek smiled as he witnessed India's first proper meal in over a week. Never a well-mannered eater, she always seemed to consider food consumption a waste of time. Now, half-starved, she was forcing mouthfuls down as quickly as her capacity to swallow, which seemed fairly high.

He noticed that Heather was watching him with an amused expression on her face. She had caught him watching India. Damn, more fuel for the fire.

"So, when are you going to tell us what you found out, India?"

"When she's had something to eat, Heather. Can't you see she's hungry?"

India stopped chewing when she realised everybody's eyes were on her. She pointed a fork at Derek. "Tell them, will you?"

"Well, this might seem a bit far-fetched—"

George leaned back in the chair and crossed his arms. "This'll be good."

"Yeah, right. It is. I guess the shortened version is the best."

"Before you start—just remind us what the helicopter was doing here to begin with."

"Yeah, good idea, George. Meg was about to have twins and there were complications."

"Who was the father?"

"We're not quite sure."

Luke coughed and Derek glared at him. "Luke thinks it might have been me."

"Might have been?" George laughed. "You can't remember?"

"To my knowledge, Meg and I never had sex, but apparently someone just like me came and impregnated her."

"Wow. That's impressive." George was still smirking.

Derek sighed. "You're making it hard for me to tell the story. Anyway, the helicopter was carrying someone who could help, but it crashed, killing all three on board."

"Okay. So India is running tests on all three?"

"Yes, and getting some results that are exciting for her and a bit overwhelming for me."

"In what way?" Heather looked puzzled.

Derek looked at India for help. She shrugged and took another mouthful of food.

"One of the victims was from the future."

The living room erupted into shrieks and laughter. A baby began crying in the bedroom. Heather swore and told everyone to hush. India smiled.

"Well, it sounded better the way India told it to me."

All eyes swivelled back to the geneticist. She pointed the fork back to Derek. "It's true. Let him talk."

"She ran a genome sequencing test on body one and compared it to the sequence of someone just before May 2013. She found some mutations."

"What sort?"

"Lots. Look, wait until she finishes eating and she can tell you herself."

Connie passed more potatoes to India, who accepted them gratefully.

"If she ever stops eating." George was smirking again. India flicked some mashed potato at him.

Connie, Luke and George began clearing the table. Dishes were washed and put away. Finally, everyone resumed their positions around the table and looked at India, who was swallowing the last mouthful of food.

She wiped her face on a sleeve and cleared her throat. "Well, it's like this." She spent the next ten minutes telling them an abbreviated version of what she'd explained to Derek in the car.

Derek was able to sit back and watch the expressions of the four other adults turn from disbelief to wonder. At the end of her talk, they looked back at Derek bug-eyed.

"Meg and I talked about that person being an alien or something. Someone who wanted to remain hidden from us." Luke frowned. "We didn't think of someone from the future."

"So they came back to help us. Why?"

"Dunno, Heather. But I'd say it was to help themselves."

"What do you mean?"

"India can tell us the mutations that have occurred in man since 2013. These have to do with health and lifestyle. The better we are now, the better they are. Especially given the tiny gene pool they will develop from."

"Wow!" Luke's eyes were dreamy. "It's like a sci-fi movie!"

"Exactly."

"What a shame he died, that dude. It would be great to meet him."

"Yeah, we could have learned a lot. It would have helped them immeasurably in the future." Derek thought for a moment. "But he didn't die in vain. Now we're thinking how we can help them."

"Howzat?" George took a swig from his whiskey glass.

"Everything we do here and now affects them in the future. If we have too much to drink," Derek nodded at George, "it affects their DNA."

George laughed. "Okay, Mr Perfect."

"Let me tell you I'm not perfect. I did a good job on myself with alcohol there for a while. Take Heather, though, who doesn't like vegetables."

"Hey! Unfair!"

"I'm just saying that we really have to think about this. We are the custodians of the future human race."

"Incredible."

"Yeah, it is. India thinks this guy came back from around four hundred years from now. What is the population? Are they surviving well? The DNA suggests they are, but I'm thinking they must have problems, because they went to a lot of trouble to help us."

George nodded. "Yeah, I see where you're coming from. Custodians of the future human race, hey? Sounds important. You'd better start breeding then, Derek. You've been a bit of a slouch in that regard. And India could start reproducing again soon."

India looked at him with distaste. Heather whacked George on the arm. "She's only just lost John," she hissed.

"Can't waste any time. We're the custodians—"

Derek groaned. It had definitely gone to George's head.

A terrible noise made Derek wake with a start. It took a few seconds to work out where he was—on the sofa of the community house. He hadn't gone home. Lying still, he listened for more sounds.

Luke and Connie's bedroom door opened and he could hear somebody shuffling toward the room where the children were sleeping. Connie's voice was low and urgent. Heather's was high and increasing in pitch.

"Oh my God! Oh my God!"

"Hush now. Shh. Don't wake the other children. We'll take her out to the living room. I don't think Derek has gone home yet."

The women appeared. Heather was carrying a bundle and her face was contorted and wet with tears.

"She was cold. I went to feed them and she was just stiff and cold."

Derek jumped up then and took the bundle from Heather's arms. He laid it on the sofa, already knowing that the child had died.

"What time did you last check on them?"

"A-About ten o'clock, when I gave them their last feed."

"Anyone know the time now?"

Connie looked outside. "It's still dark but I think sunrise isn't far off."

"What position was this one lying in?"

Heather looked confused for a moment. "Um, I don't know. I can't think—" She was beginning to shiver violently.

"Connie, grab Heather a blanket would you? Maybe a hot drink as well."

Luke came out, scratching his head. "What's up?" He saw Heather's face and Derek leaning over the motionless child. He turned on his heel and went to find Connie.

Derek began undoing the baby's clothing. "She was the bigger of the twins. What did you name her?"

"Prue. I thought she was healthy." The sobs began again.

"Yes, I thought so, too." He examined every part of the baby's body, cupping her head in the palm of his hand as he turned her over. His handling of her was gentle but efficient.

As he was conducting the examination an owl began calling. Its croak resembled that of a frog's. The interval between calls was only a few seconds and it repeated over and over. To Derek, trying to concentrate, it had the effect of nails scraping a blackboard.

Finally he shook his head and began replacing the clothing. He was standing not far from Heather and George's bedroom. The door was shut. How was George sleeping through all the commotion? Derek's knuckles made a sharp rapping sound on the solid wood. "George! Wake up George!"

"You'll need to do better than that." Heather's tone through the tears was bitter. "He was on the whiskey again. He woke me with his snoring and that's when I went to feed the babies."

Derek sighed. It was a shame there was so much alcohol still left in so many locations in and around Maleny. He himself often thought of calling in to a hotel and helping himself to a shot or two. He felt the need now.

"Here we go." Connie was carrying blankets and a hot water bottle. Derek could see signs that she'd been crying and was trying hard to control herself for Heather's sake. "Sit down, lovie. There we are. That's better, isn't it?" Her eyes were as big as saucers as she looked at Derek and the inert baby, and they held a question.

"There's no obvious cause of death. I'll have to investigate further tomorrow."

Connie looked at Heather. "Do you want to hold her for a moment—say goodbye?" Heather nodded. Connie walked to the sofa and straightened the baby's clothing, taking care to make sure everything was perfect. She gently handed the baby to its mother and stood with her hand on Heather's shoulder for a moment. Then she went and barged into the bedroom where George was sleeping.

Derek and Heather heard George exclaiming noisily with slurred speech. Connie walked back through the living room to the kitchen. She filled a jug with water and carried back in to the bedroom. There was a splash and more complaints by George. Connie spoke to him in low tones. There was silence. Connie returned, closing the door behind her. "George will be out in a moment, Heather."

"No, I think I'll take Prue in there. She can lie with us for a little while."

As Heather carried the dead infant into the bedroom, Connie looked enquiringly at Derek.

"I don't know——truly I don't. Could be SIDS."

"Could be what?"

"Sudden Infant Death Syndrome. Cot death."

"Oh." Connie's face began crumpling again. "Such a tiny wee thing. It's just awful."

"I'll look at her in the morning, but based on what I

saw just now, I'm not sure I'm going to be able to tell much more."

"Please try hard. It would help to know. It's heartbreaking."

"Yes, and we need more children, not less."

Luke walked in and folded Connie in his arms. She buried her face in his chest and began sobbing. Luke smoothed her hair and whispered in her ear.

When she quietened, they listened to the muffled voices coming from the bedroom. There was the rumbling of George's words and the higher, distressed tones of Heather's. Time passed slowly. The voices stopped.

Connie sighed and looked at Derek. "Should I go and take the baby now—put her somewhere?"

"I'll do that. You and Luke should go back to bed."

Derek couldn't move. He sat and listened to Connie walking quietly into the children's bedroom. After a few minutes she went back into hers. She and Luke spoke for a few minutes. Bedclothes rustled. The house fell silent.

After a few minutes he went back into Heather and George's room. Heather was sitting in a chair, the same one that Derek had seen Meg seated in so long ago. She had the baby clasped to her chest and was rocking backward and forwards. George was sitting on the bed in front of Heather, his hand resting on her leg and a dazed expression on his face. Their silence felt like a vacuum.

"I'll take her now. You two had better try to get some more sleep."

Heather shook her head. "Sleep? I don't think so." She leaned over and kissed Prue's forehead. Tears dripped onto the child. "I'm glad you were here. Take her now. I'm going to check on the other children." She stood and passed the bundle to Derek. Her robe swirled as she turned and ran out of the room.

Derek cradled the child in his arms and looked at George. "Are you okay, mate?" George didn't turn, but just shrugged his shoulders without saying a word. "Okay, well I'll examine her in the morning and we'll talk again after that."

"It's not really my field, you know." India was pushing her glasses further up her nose.

"I know, but I thought perhaps you might see something I missed."

"Are you going to do a full autopsy?"

Derek looked around the portable hospital. There was enough equipment to conduct one, but he hesitated.

"No, I don't think so. That would be distressing for all concerned. Most of all me."

"Hmm. I guess so."

"There's no sign of distress. No discolouration. No rashes or bites. I'm at a bit of a loss."

"SIDS?"

"Could well be. A healthy baby dies in its sleep without reason. It fits."

"At least it can be something to tell Heather."

"Yeah. Poor thing. She'll want answers."

"Should we bury her today?"

"I can't see why not."

"There will be three in the graveyard now. Meg, John and Prue."

"That's not a good thing."

"No."

"I'll check out the other kiddies this afternoon, I think."

"Could be wise."

"Yeah, just the basics. I don't want to frighten the other parents too much."

India laughed. "Like me?"

Derek looked at her and blinked. "Yes, sorry India. I forgot."

"That's okay. Sometimes I forget too."

"Yes, you do, don't you?"

"At least you don't judge me too harshly."

"Not at all. It takes all kinds. I've seen a lot worse mothers than you."

"Gee, thanks!"

"You know what I mean."

"Yeah, I suppose I do. Heather and Connie still want me to have more children, though. Have hinted that they'll take over the parenting." India snorted.

"Their motives are good."

"I know. It's just—"

"What?"

"The whole pregnancy thing just seems unnatural to me. You know that movie where Sigourney Weaver has that alien growing inside her?"

"My God. That bad?" Derek flashed a rare smile.

"Yeah. That bad."

"Must have seemed like a long pregnancy."

"Well, I wasn't too healthy, either. I'd been on my own all that time."

"I suppose you were as thin as you are now."

"Thinner!"

"You're healthier now."

"Yeah. Do you think I should have more children?"

"Does my opinion matter?"

India shrugged and turned away. "I guess you'd have to be the father."

Derek didn't say anything for a few seconds, but waited for the sick feeling to subside. The thought of starting a new family always caused that in him. How could he do that to Sophie and the kids?

He knew he had to choose his words very carefully. India was busying herself, putting the medical equipment in a neat pile on the bench, avoiding his gaze.

"Yes, there's that. It's not out of the question, but we might just think about this for a while." A thought came to him and he gave a half-smile. "Besides, I'd like to tease Heather, Connie and George for a while longer yet."

The mood of the adults at the burial wasn't helped by misty rain. Plump drops fell from the branches of the fig tree. Heather's sobs echoed around the property as Derek said a few words about the baby girl. He found this hard—hadn't had much to do with her since he had guided her into the world and passed her to George. Now he felt guilty about that.

Religion wasn't playing a part in their lives at the community. None of the survivors belonged to any organised religious group. George labelled himself an atheist, but the others were uncomfortable with that term and were content to claim they just weren't inclined toward formal religion.

As Luke filled the grave with dirt and they began walking back to the house, Derek wondered idly if some sort of religious faith would be of comfort to Heather—everlasting life and all that. He dismissed the thought with a shrug. He was a man of science, after all. Perhaps he'd ask India about it later.

Connie had prepared a cake and some sandwiches, and there was tea and coffee waiting. Thomas and Maisie, the two oldest of the children, fell on the cake with cries of delight, and Connie reprimanded them gently. Heather had gone into her bedroom and closed the door behind her. George wandered over to the detailed map hanging on the wall and peered at it intently.

Derek was quick to join him. He pointed to a dot in the northwest that was marked with a piece of sticky note, cut into an arrow. "This is where I reckon the hospital is."

"Really? That's a long way north."

"Hmm. I know. Meg only knew they were flying inland and didn't really have much idea other than that."

"Women haven't got a bloody clue about direction, have they? Luke didn't know?"

"He was too busy with Connie and the two kids."

"So, when are you planning on leaving?"

"It's been put off for too long. Something always seems to stop me. I'll prepare everything today and tomorrow. I think I'll leave the day after that, at first light."

"Okay—sounds like a plan. Luke and I will give the four-wheel-drive a going over this afternoon."

"Thanks, mate. Would you mind gassing it up as well and also filling the jerry cans?"

"Not a problem. God, I wish I was going. Sure you don't want me along?"

Derek smiled. "I'd love the company, but you're needed here."

"Bummer. Okay."

Connie walked toward the men, carrying steaming cups. "Here we are. Just what's needed on a day like this."

"Great, thanks." Derek watched George turn around to add a shot of whiskey to the coffee. He became aware of Connie still standing next to him.

"India thought you might be examining the children later this afternoon."

Derek looked closely at Connie. He could sense her fear, knew she was concerned about her own children. "Yeah, I thought I'd give them all a quick going over. How about in an hour or so?"

Connie nodded. "I'll have them ready for you."

The DVD began repeating the movie Derek had been watching. It hadn't been a thought provoking or visually satisfying film, but it had helped pass the time and keep him awake.

He had volunteered to stay the night at the community house in an attempt to ease Heather and Connie's nervousness. The problem with being an overly sensitive man was that he was constantly aware of the feelings and emotions of those around him. He had sensed that the two women were strung tight emotionally and wanted him to stay. Promising to check on the children through the night meant they could sleep in peace. He even offered to deliver the surviving twin to Heather when it was time for feeding.

He rifled through the other DVDs in the box, and was pleased to find an old art-house movie that he'd seen several times, but still enjoyed. He loaded the DVD into the disk tray and slid it shut. Some images began flashing on the screen, and he pressed the fast-forward button. When it came to the start of the movie, he pressed pause and went into the kitchen.

He was rummaging through the pantry looking for snacks when he heard a door closing and the shuffling of feet.

George appeared in the kitchen, scratching his head and his testicles at the same time. "Hey. I need water. Huge thirst."

"Alcohol does that."

"Yeah, I know that, mate. Thanks for reminding me. Whatcha doing?"

"Passing the time. Watching DVD's. Eating. Might make some hot chocolate. Want some?"

"Hey, yeah."

Derek began pouring milk into a saucepan. "While that's heating up, come into the kids' room with me. I want to show you what to watch out for while I'm gone on the trip west."

"What, you reckon I'm going to get up in the middle of the night?"

"Just for a few nights, until everything calms down."

"I'll need a nap through the day then."

Derek held his finger to his lips as they approached the children's room. The door was always left open to allow as much ventilation as possible. Four beds, four cots and two cradles were arranged dormitory-style. One cradle was empty. "Try not to disturb them, but make sure none have rolled onto their bellies." Derek was whispering as he leaned over each child and placed his hand against their chests to check for the rise and fall of breath. "If they are sleeping on their stomachs, turn them onto their sides." He arrived at the second cot and leaned over. "It's easy to tell if they're okay." He frowned. His hand was on the child's chest, but he began to move it around quickly. He brought his other arm over the edge of the cot and scooped the child up. "Damn. Damn. Damn."

He ran into the dining room, followed by a puzzled George. "She's not breathing, mate." He placed her on the table and loosened her pink nightie. He put his ear to her chest. "Get India."

George shuffled off while Derek tilted the child's head back and peered into her mouth checking for obstructions. This girl was older than Prue—one of Connie's children. He calculated her age and considered the best method of resuscitation. He began puffing into her mouth with quick breaths. He paused and checked to see if she'd begun breathing. Moving more urgently, he began compressing the breastbone rhythmically. There was still no response. He began breathing into her mouth again.

India appeared by his side, her calm presence already helping. Derek pointed to the child's head. "You puff five times gently into her mouth while holding the nose. Repeat that five times, then I'll do the chest compressions." India nodded and began. Soon it was Derek's turn.

They paused while Derek checked for any signs of life. None. "Let's do it again."

The owl that sounded like a frog began croaking again, just as it had the night before. Derek tried to block the annoying sound from his consciousness. He and India repeated the resuscitation cycle over and over again for nearly half an hour. Finally Derek stood back, his shoulders sagging. "We got to her too late. I can't believe I checked her too late!"

India looked at him sternly. "I can't believe you'd find a way to blame yourself for this."

"I was on watch."

"Nonsense. I'd better go and wake Luke and Connie."

"I should be the one."

"No." India looked at him searchingly, a gaze that took in the tremor beginning in his hands and the colour receding from his face. "Just sit down for a minute. Let them sleep in peace for a while longer while you have a chance to calm yourself." He was shaking visibly by then and could feel the bile rising in his throat. India saw George still hovering in the doorway watching helplessly. "Get a bowl from the kitchen, would you George? A big one, or even a bucket. Quickly!"

George rushed back with a yellow plastic bucket that India placed between Derek's knees. As he retched, India sat quietly by his side. "Perhaps a glass of water now, George.

Thanks."

Derek sipped the water and then smiled crookedly at India. "Now you know my secret. Normally it takes a bit longer to happen—after I've talked to the parents."

"It's no big deal, Derek. A lot of medical professionals suffer the same thing. It means you're human. I'd rather have my children cared for by a sensitive doctor than one with no feelings. Do you think you can handle it now?"

"In a sec." He rinsed his mouth with water and spat into the bucket. He walked back over to the table. "This is Krystal. She was just over twelve months old."

"Yeah, Connie said they had a party for the twins not long before we first came here."

George was still hovering and looking toward his bedroom door as though planning an escape.

"Stay on hand will you George? We'll need some support for Luke and Connie."

George's eyes darted sideways. "Maybe I should get Heather."

"No. Leave her sleep. She's exhausted after last night and today."

"It happened to me too, you know. I'm really tired."

"Yes, but you're already awake. And these people need you." India was talking in a no-nonsense tone that George responded to. He sat down meekly. India looked at Derek again, noting the steady hands and better colour. She took a deep breath and went to wake the dead child's parents.

"She's just the same as Prue. I can't find a cause of death."

For the second time in two days, Derek and India leaned over the operating table in the portable hospital. The generator was working noisily, providing electricity for the large light that shone on the child.

"So she was fine when you checked her over with the other kids yesterday afternoon? No symptoms however minor?"

"Nothing."

"We have to check for something. The brain or heart? Lungs or liver?"

Derek raised his hands and let them fall. "We can, but I don't know."

"This may not end here. What about the other children? I think we have to try."

"Yes. Yes, you're right. Are you okay with assisting?"

"Of course."

"You understand that I'm not really qualified. I may not recognise a fault if I see it."

"Sure, but we can weigh the organs and take blood samples. We can check for clots—"

"I guess we could then find a book at the library."

"Or a university..."

"Yeah. Okay then—where should we start?"

"Liver, heart and kidneys. They are the easiest to get to."

They worked in grim silence for half an hour. Finally, Derek stood back and removed his gloves.

"All we can tell Luke and Connie is that there was nothing wrong with Krystal as far as we could determine, but that we will continue to investigate."

"Poor people. It would have been good to be able to give them a cause of death. I don't know how Connie's going recover from losing this one." She looked down at the child and covered her with a sheet. "Her grief is so intense she can barely talk. Or cry. She just sits and stares. And Luke's way of coping with the loss is talking non-stop. He talks and talks."

"To think he used to be mute."

"He was expounding quite a theory this morning, after you went home to get changed."

"Oh?"

"Says there's a force trying to get rid of us. Like the snakes."

Derek snorted. "Meg wrote something similar in her journals. There was the bushfire and then the cyclone. The wild dogs were out to get her too."

"Do you think she was right?"

Derek thought for a moment. "She wasn't a woman prone to hysteria. Not quite as calm as you, but sensible."

"So there could be some truth in it?"

"How will we ever know?"

"I don't know. Perhaps we'll just see all of us picked off one by one. What can we expect next? Stinging insects? Poisoned water?"

"The snakes did act unusually, and they weren't our normal native snakes."

India looked at him levelly. "Perhaps it's time you really concentrated on getting those answers you've been talking about."

"Yes, it's time I headed out west. Here's the plan. We'll weigh and photograph the organs and take some tissue and blood samples. Then we'll have the burial later this morning."

"Yeah, okay."

"I'll leave straight after that. The sun will be in my eyes, but I can get a few hours driving done at least."

"How far is it, exactly?"

"Remember I'm not sure this is the right place yet. I

won't know until I get there."

"But if it is?"

"Fifteen-hundred kilometres. My back is a problem at the moment, and I reckon six hours a day will be all I can stand."

"So three days to get there. I hope it's the right place."

Derek rolled his eyes. "I hope so too."

"I should be there with you."

"Yes, definitely. I wish you could be spared from here. You know, I don't even know what I'm looking for—I'm just desperate to find anything. Another set of eyes would really help."

"I'll make myself useful here. I'll find some texts on autopsies and see if I can discover anything."

"I hope you find one specifically for infants."

"I'll find one. I'll also have to help Heather and Connie while they recover from all of this." She looked at Derek searchingly. "Are you okay? You still seem a bit off."

He dropped his gaze. "It's just all a bit much, you know? One thing after another."

"Were you better when you lived alone at Noosaville?"

Derek leaned back against the table and crossed his arms. "No, not really." He laughed without humour. "I'm beyond repair, I think."

"Then maybe a drive into the desert is just what you need."

"I hope so. I really do."

CHAPTER NINE

Around ten kilometres west of Hughenden, on an unmarked road that turned off the Flinders Highway, was a dot on the map which was marked with an icon that suggested it was a hospital or medical centre. As Derek came to a stop outside this building, he frowned. Could this be the place? It seemed so small.

His own memories of the hospital were vague at best. All he remembered was the dormitory he stayed in and the view from a high window. The terrain was certainly similar—flat, dry and scrubby.

Why would anyone build a hospital in such a remote location? To treat members of the various Aboriginal tribes that inhabited the area? Maybe the owners and workers on remote cattle stations?

He remembered Meg's description of an airstrip they landed on in their small jet, and how she'd remarked about the lack of signage. Then they had a short drive by bus over an unsealed road. He could go looking for the airstrip, but decided to check the building out first.

As his feet touched the ground, he groaned and clutched his back. Three days of driving had taken their toll on his lower spine, and he had to stop and perform a series of stretches before he could walk. Finally, he was able to hobble to the hospital entrance.

The interior was cool and dark, and as his eyes adjusted, he saw he was standing in what looked like a reception area. Several doors opened from that point. The first led to a treatment room. The second was to an operating theatre. A third revealed an office. He held his breath and opened the fourth. There was a short hallway with two doors. Both opened into nearly identical dormitories. He stood in the second and nodded his head slowly. Yes, this was the place.

He was hot, tired, and dusty. He needed water and anti-inflammatory medication. He craved a decent meal washed down with an ice cold beer.

He lowered himself onto one of the narrow dormitory beds and stared at the ceiling. His thoughts went immediately to Maleny, and he worried about what was happening there. Connie's tear-stained face appeared, her appalling, fathomless grief heartbreaking to him. She had been inconsolable after Krystal's death and even Luke, struggling with his own grief, was at a loss when it came to trying to help her.

Derek's own efforts were clumsy at best. His pronouncement that the cause of death was 'probably SIDS' caused Connie to start pounding him on the chest. "I don't want to hear what it 'probably' was. I want to hear the truth! Someone or something is stealing our children's lives, one by one!"

It was decided that each adult would stay awake and watch over the children on a roster system. They would check that none were sleeping on their stomachs. From time to time they would check that each child's breathing was regular. Two hours each, every night.

George had promised to limit his drinking to two standard shots per night, so he could be alert for his shift. Derek remembered the look in Heather's eyes when she said, "You've promised. Break this and you'll be in trouble." George had looked suitably solemn.

Two nights had passed since he had driven away, waving to India who was standing on the verandah. He wished he could just pick up a mobile telephone and call.

Connie had issued some commands. "Find out what's happening for Christ's sake, Derek. Find some clues. Those ones who helped us, I know they died in the helicopter crash but there must be more of them. Find them. They might help us save the other children."

"We don't know that the other kids are going to be affected. Let's not worry about what may not happen."

"Oh, I'll worry all right. You just go and find out the truth."

"There may not be anything to find out."

"Do your best."

As he looked around the dormitory of the remote hospital, he was aware of the walls turning pink. The sun was setting. He should get up and organise himself. He'd just have a short rest first.

There was a low, rhythmic sound. Derek became aware of the vibrations in his chest first, before his ears picked up the strange melody which seemed to consist of several notes that were repeated over and over.

The sunset-lit walls were gone. Now there was darkness and flickering light—orange and red. This light danced about the ceiling, daring to be chased. Derek rose unsteadily and decided to investigate.

The sound, which he now realised was a didgeridoo, echoed through Derek's head, and he couldn't stop the vibrations resonating through his body. A didgeridoo needed a person to play it—usually an Aboriginal person. The flickering light was from a fire. What was happening outside?

He had woken shivering, and now tore a blanket from the bed and wrapped it around himself. He dragged a chair to the high window and leaned it against the wall. Stepping onto the chair, he was surprised to find there was no pain in his back. Surprised and relieved.

There was a fire. It was burning in a contained area, several metres from the four-wheel-drive. There was a figure behind it, sitting cross-legged, but this person wasn't playing the didgeridoo. He was hitting two short pieces of wood together.

Derek climbed down from the chair and made his way out the front doors of the hospital. Derek sensed that the figure in the darkness knew he was there but didn't openly acknowledge it. Derek approached slowly from the darkness until he too was encircled by the firelight. Only then did the other man indicate with his head that Derek should sit.

The didgeridoo was being played from the darkness behind the Aboriginal man. This man was of an advanced age, with a grey beard and hair. The beard was long and unkempt, the hair short and kinky. Even by the firelight, Derek could tell that the old man's skin was dry like leather.

Derek slowly became aware of the sky and the spectacle of the brilliant stars. He almost gasped out loud.

There was no moon on this night, so the stars had the entire stage to themselves.

The music stopped. The man's hands stilled, the sticks lying inert in his lap. He began talking in a low voice which mimicked the rhythm of the now silent didgeridoo.

"In the Dreamtime, the Rainbow Serpent was big boss fella—wandered all around here." The man used both arms to sweep across the broad expanse of land. "It made things, good things: mountains, waterholes, rivers, and ridges. It was the creator. It created the world and was the keeper of water. It lives in water now. A water-hole long ways that way." He pointed to the northwest.

"We fella—we had the stories. We passed them father to son, father to daughter, mother to son, mother to daughter since Dreamtime. Big stories."

Derek nodded. The man was silent for several minutes.

"Stories—like songs. Sang 'em when walking. Walked like the Rainbow Serpent—the same way. The stories told what the Rainbow Serpent fella made. We walked same paths and songs they tell where the Rainbow Serpent fella created things. Waterholes of big fish. Plants. Caves. The songlines. We fella walked the songlines and sang the songs."

He nodded and was silent again.

"When we fella walked the songlines, created the world

just like the Rainbow Serpent fella did. Every time walked the songlines, world was new again. We knew when to burn the land and hunt. We got bark off trees, didn't cut trees down."

Derek adjusted his weight. He didn't want to move too much and interrupt the story.

"But then the bad came. Booze. Fencing. Cattle. Men said they owned the land. Said we couldn't be on it. Put too much cattle on it. Ruined it. Ruined the people with the booze and drugs."

The man was breathing deeply. His voice trembled.

"The stories lost. Sons and daughters went to big cities. Others stayed but they were no good. They were lost. No one to walk the songlines. No one to make the world new. The Rainbow Serpent fella he moved again. This time he was angry fella."

Derek wanted to ask what happened next, but found he couldn't talk. He waited for the man to continue.

"When the Rainbow Serpent fella angry, bad things happen."

Derek felt a chill race up and down his back. There was foreboding in those words.

"Rainbow Serpent got rid of bad fella. Us. We were parasite. He got rid of us. But two lived. Boy-man and girl."

Two? Derek frowned.

"Rainbow Serpent, he big fella. Need to keep him happy. He boss man of all this." The man waved his arms around again. Then his voice dropped. "Tread softly on land. Boy-man and girl new keepers. Need help."

The didgeridoo began its rhythmic music again, but this time it came from Derek's left. He peered into the darkness, trying to find the source of the sound. When he turned back to the fire, he found he was alone. The music stopped again.

The Aboriginal man's words echoed in Derek's head, over and over. "When the Rainbow Serpent gets angry, bad things happen."

When Derek woke, it was to a brand new day. The sun was high and he felt rested. He moved his legs from side to side in the narrow bed, testing his lower back. The pain returned with a vengeance, and he groaned.

A memory came back to him in a flash. He was stepping onto a chair and then sitting cross-legged on the ground with no pain. His memory of the meeting with the Aboriginal elder had a dreamlike quality. Was it real?

The blanket was on the bed, spread evenly over him. Had he wrapped it around himself and then later replaced it neatly? Or was the whole episode a figment of his imagination?

He hadn't had such powerful and realistic dreams since—when? When he was being led to Maleny. Dreams were being planted in his mind. This one was just like those.

Irritation rose in him. If someone, somewhere, was trying to tell him something, then they'd better just come and talk to him in person.

His next emotion was worry about the community in Maleny. He should be with them. He shouldn't be on this wild goose chase. There was nothing to see. The hospital was empty. He had failed. All he had to show for three days of wasted effort was a dream.

"When the Rainbow Serpent gets angry, bad things happen."

He sat on the side of the bed with his head cradled in open hands. He wasn't good on his own—felt the need to be back with the others. Felt that he could go mad out there on the edge of the desert with his weird dreams.

"Okay." He was talking out loud, his voice croaking. "Okay, you bastards. I'm telling you once and for all." The volume of his voice was rising. "If you have something to say to me, come and say it."

He walked out through the reception area to the front of the building and looked skyward.

"Here I am! If you want to give me a message, COME AND GIVE IT TO ME! I'VE HAD ENOUGH OF YOUR GAMES!"

He was panting. How long since he'd had water, or even food? He opened the car door and reached into the refrigerator. India had scrambled to put some food together for him, but it wasn't the quality of Connie's. He chewed on a stale sandwich and drank thirstily from a container of Maleny water.

The silence of the desert, on this particular morning, was extraordinary. It was like a vacuum. Derek closed his eyes and listened intently. Not a sound.

He leaned against the vehicle, and considered the building in front of him. He would search it thoroughly this morning. If he found nothing by the time the sun was high in the sky, he would leave. He would dose up on pain-killers and drive back to Maleny quickly—three days was way too long —and see what was happening.

That was a good plan.

Derek steered the vehicle back onto the Flinders Highway, glad to be on a sealed road again. Most of the major highways were still in reasonable condition—there were some washed-out sections and large potholes that he had to watch for, but he knew he could maintain a steady speed.

In the township of Hughenden he took Stansfield Street to view the Muttaburrasaurus replica which was constructed of fibreglass. He felt a surge of boyish enthusiasm, fuelled by the almost slavish obsession he'd had with dinosaurs at around the age of ten.

East of Hughenden was a sign to Mount Walker. It was only thirteen kilometres out of his way, and he had a sudden strong desire to see it. Instead of taking the dogleg left on the A6, he took the Hughenden-Muttaburra Road and drove for several minutes until he saw the signpost to the Mount Walker Lookout.

The mountain itself was small and steep. The road to the summit was sealed but in bad condition. The incline was harsh, and Derek was grateful for the off-road capabilities of the vehicle.

He reached the lookout and shook his head in wonder. A three hundred and sixty degree view of the surrounding area was unhindered. The flat plains rolled out in every direction, red and dry. A sign told him that he was standing four hundred and seventy-eight metres above sea level. Amazing.

There was a park bench at the most scenic point of the lookout, and Derek lowered himself slowly on to it. Closing his eyes, he tried to tune in to his surroundings—listen to the world. There wasn't much to be heard.

Meg's journal had told of the summit lookouts she would stand at, all the way up the eastern seaboard of Australia, on her journey north. He saw now why she chose to do this—understood the desire to search for signs of life. His eyes remained closed as he tried to envisage her on Mount Walker—a place she'd never visited, to his knowledge.

"Stunning view, isn't it?"

Derek's eyes flew open, and he turned quickly to his left. A man, old and wrinkled, was sitting beside him.

"Where the hell did you come from?"

"Hi. I'm Martin." He held out his hand.

"Derek." Martin's handshake was strong. "Who are you? What are you doing way out here?"

"Oh that's easy to answer. You called; I came."

"Hey?"

"You called out for me to come and talk to you in person. Here I am."

"But—"

"Sorry, I've surprised you."

"Um, yes."

"We've tried different ways of communicating with you, but nothing seems to work well. You wanted the direct approach, so here I am."

"The Aboriginal man last night?"

"Yes, that was us."

"Who's us?"

"Just people trying to help you. I brought something for your back, by the way." He had been holding a device in his left hand and now showed it to Derek. "Lean forward." Derek could feel the cool surface of the machine being held to his lower spine. There was increasing heat and vibrations. This lasted less than a minute. "There, done."

Derek rotated in the seat. No pain. He lifted his legs. He stood. "Wow. How long does that last for?"

"Oh, it's fixed."

"Eh?"

"All done. All fixed."

"Forever?"

"Well, yes. As long as you don't do anything to give yourself a major injury."

Tears swelled in his eyes. A life without back pain. Was it possible?

The man motioned him back onto the seat. "I guess you have some questions for me."

Boy, did he have some questions.

CHAPTER TEN

Derek looked at Martin carefully, noting some interesting features. His head was slightly larger at the top than normal, and when Derek looked at Martin's eyes, he saw that they were an unusual colour—indescribable. If he had to say what colour they were, he'd say greenish, bluish, violet. Like nothing he'd seen before.

"I guess you're from another time. The future." Derek felt an immature embarrassment from even saying these words.

"Well done!" Martin smiled.

"How far into the future?"

"Around five hundred years."

"Ah, okay. I was set to drive back to Maleny quickly, but felt the need to come here. Did you do that?"

"Yes."

Derek waited for him to elaborate but there was nothing else forthcoming. "So, the Aboriginal man last night said there were two survivors in May 2013—a boy-man and a girl."

"Yes. I am descended from them."

"But—"

"Luke and Connie. They were the only survivors."

"What about the rest of us?"

"This is where it becomes a bit complicated."

"Before you start, what's going on in Maleny? I'm worried."

"All okay. No more deaths."

"Great. So the rest of us..."

"We weren't doing well—in the future. Our health was bad. There weren't many of us and we weren't strong."

"So?"

"We found a way of returning. It's very limited—each person can only do it a few times. The windows of opportunity are narrow. Today was almost accidental."

"Wow."

"Indeed."

"How long will you stay for?"

"Not long."

Derek was becoming frustrated. Realising he was asking the wrong questions, he changed tack.

"So Luke and Connie survived. How did the rest of us come into the picture?"

"We found out what killed everyone and made a vaccine."

"What was it? That's one thing I really need to know. What killed my wife and children?"

"The polar ice caps were melting. There was a virus that thawed and became active again for the first time in millennia."

"A virus that affected humans—in the ice caps?"

"No, this one didn't affect humans immediately. It mutated."

"But I don't understand how it killed everyone at almost the same time."

"It didn't. Not initially. It affected a few people first, but the authorities were slow to react. They didn't realise what they were dealing with. It took a small hold, then flashed across the world."

"Incredible. So you created a vaccine?"

"Yes. A colleague of mine came back and inoculated two people: Meg and you."

"Why us?"

"We didn't know who to save, had no idea. We found an old database of a firm that did psychometric testing. Meg was a standout in terms of capability and flexibility. You were caring, sensitive and had skills we admired. We needed someone to look after the children. We wanted healthy offspring so that we would be healthier in the future."

"I see. So there were two of us to start with, selected for our psychological profiles and other skills. You went back in time to before May 2013 and inoculated us without our knowledge."

"That's correct."

"But then there were three brothers....evil sorts..."

Martin sighed. "Don't remind me. A colleague—William—did that. Bad mistake."

"You're not wrong. Meg fixed that mistake for you."

"She's a good girl."

"Not anymore."

"She still lives."

"Really, where?"

"We didn't want her to die the way she did. It was our fault. The best we could do was transport her backwards."

"Oh, so—"

"It gets a bit messy. She actually ended up..."

"Yeah?"

"Never mind. She's all right."

"But I saw her!"

"How do you mean?"

"Well, not exactly. It was like— thin veil of her."

"Describe it to me."

Martin listened intently while Derek described the time he'd seen Meg at the library, and then again outside the house in Maleny. Derek noticed Martin's face turning grim.

"That's not good news. We're doing damage with all this backwards and forwards in time."

"What sort of damage?"

"We're causing bleeds in the fabric that separates... oh, you needn't bother yourself about that. We'll fix it. You have more pressing concerns."

Derek shook his head. He didn't understand but he had many more questions.

"So then there is India, Heather and George."

"And John. Poor man."

"I guess you came back again and gave them vaccine—for more people to help?"

"Yes, we needed a geneticist, an educator, a builder and an environmental expert."

"You picked well."

"John was a sad loss though."

"These attacks—bushfire, cyclone, snakes, sickness, child-deaths—what are they all about?"

"We don't have all the answers. It seems like one of two things. The earth is trying to rid itself of the remaining humans, or everyone except Luke and Connie."

"I see." Derek mused for a moment. "The Rainbow Serpent was angry?"

"Call it what you will. I'm sure the American Indians have another name for such a spirit, and other cultures as well. Let's just say that Mother Nature got fed up. You can probably relate to that best."

"Yes. I see now."

"And unless you show an effort in making the world a better place, she will keep trying to rid herself of you."

"Got it. That's why John was such a bad loss. The environmentalist."

"Yes, but I'm sure you and the others can research some best practises."

"I suppose so."

"Let's get out of this sun. My skin isn't used to UV rays. Let's eat something in the shelter over there."

The man moved slowly, and Derek wondered if he should offer help. Finally they sat down in the shade. Martin reached into his coat and produced a glass phial, which he uncorked and tipped down his throat.

Derek pulled the last of the food from the refrigerator in the vehicle. He was embarrassed to offer it to Martin, but there was nothing else. He needn't have worried. Martin waved his hands and said he'd just eaten, the contents of the phial being good enough, apparently.

Derek chewed on a vegemite and cheese sandwich, washing each mouthful down with water.

"Tell me about the two guys, the twins who flew the helicopter."

"Hmm. Another stuff-up by William, that colleague of mine. We knew we were limited in how many times we could come back, so he tried to clone some DNA of an individual living before 2013. The results were awful. It cost William his life when they crashed the helicopter."

"They were on their way to help Meg."

"Yes. Terrible day for all of us."

Derek was just beginning to get a picture of how things stood. The veil of ignorance was lifting.

"Was Meg carrying my twins?"

"Yes. We knew you didn't want to reproduce. We tried impregnating her with your semen at the hospital."

"My semen? When did you get that?"

"When we inoculated you." Martin saw Derek's colour rise. "Sorry, but you know—"

"I know that you really had no consideration for my feelings in this!"

"We were limited in opportunities and time. We had to

do what we considered was the best thing—"

"Without my knowledge or consent!"

"But anyway, she aborted the foetuses. Then we thought we'd try it the old-fashioned way."

"So, how did you manage that?"

"You were in need of medical attention after the cyclone. We brought you to the hospital here and as soon as you were stabilised we took over your controls for a while."

"How did you do that?"

"Not very well. That was also the work of William. It had the desired effect, however."

"So again you used me without my consent. Used me for your breeding purposes. You're making me quite angry, you know."

"Think of the bigger picture."

Derek took some deep breaths. "So this William was coming back to this time quite often."

"No, he'd set himself up here, because as I said, we're limited in how many times we can time travel."

"He should have just come and lived with us."

Martin shrugged. "It was his call. That's the way he wanted to do it. He thought that living among you could be dangerous in terms of what he might change. It could have catastrophic consequences back in our time."

"Perhaps you should come with me now and live with us, but be careful."

"No, in fact I have to leave very soon, my time travelling days are over."

"I see."

"And I have to get back to my present before then. We don't have much more time."

"Bummer."

"Indeed. Do you have any more questions?"

"Yes. Can you return me?"

"How do you mean?"

"Can you take me back to May 13th without the vaccine?"

"Why? We saved your life!"

"Yes, and I guess you'd expect gratitude in return."

"I would have thought so."

"I don't know how to explain this—but I'll just tell you that I died that night anyway. I died with my wife Sophie and my two kids."

"I don't understand."

"They were everything to me. Sophie was, she was just the other half of me. My heart was her heart and vice-versa. When she died, I died."

"Is that why you won't mate with anyone else?"

"The thought repels me. Makes me feel physically ill."

"I see."

"So can you?"

Martin sighed. "We need you for a bit longer."

"How much longer?"

"I don't know. It's complicated. We'll have to look at all the repercussions of you not being at Maleny."

"Like?"

"You won't lead the evil brothers to Meg. They might stay loose and cause all sorts of problems."

"They'll probably die without reproducing because they won't find Connie, Heather or India."

"Maybe."

Derek became animated. "Hey, Meg won't die! I won't have been there to impregnate her!"

"True, and that will save us a trip back to fix that."

"Also, your colleague won't have his helicopter crash! Meg won't need his help!"

Martin's eyebrows raised and he whistled.

"See?" Derek was excited.

"But then we won't have had this conversation. I feel it is important." Martin sounded dejected.

"Have it with Meg. She will understand."

"So, you want to die with your wife and children.

Maybe it can be done." He began wriggling in his seat. "I've only got a few more minutes. Can you just listen to me for that time?" Derek nodded.

"Tell the others whatever you want, but what we need is for all of you to consider the future. In five hundred years from now, we live longer but our health isn't wonderful. You know it's improved, though, since we got all of you to help Luke and Connie."

"Improved? Already?"

"Of course. Everything we do here now, helps us in the time I come from. We get India working on genetics and we improve. Just having Meg drive Luke to rescue Connie made us feel better."

"I don't understand."

"Picture this. Luke is a mess. He is a young man, alone. He knows he has to get to Cairns. He starts walking and cycling and using all means available to him, but it's seventeen hundred kilometres. By the time he gets there he is near death. Connie is near death. This actually alters their genes. Ask India about that."

"So instead, he spends a few days with Meg and regains his strength." Derek was catching on. "She ends up driving him to Cairns. Connie is sick and dehydrated, but Meg is resourceful and knows what to do. Both Luke and Connie are in better states of health."

"Exactly." Martin looks pleased. "They are able to reproduce more quickly. Their offspring are healthier."

"So, immediately, you guys in the future feel better?"

"Yes!" Martin slapped a hand on his thigh. "So now India needs to do a lot of genetic work quickly. Heather needs to start teaching the children from an early age about things that will help them live in a sustainable manner. Luke and Connie need to keep having children, but with care for Connie's health."

"What else?"

"Someone should impregnate India. Soon. You, or George, or Luke. You would be best. We need your caring personality to offset her unemotional one. If the thought of that repels you, do it by remote means."

"Remote means?"

Martin was becoming more agitated. He stood up. "In vitro—she'll know what to do. If you do that, I'll promise to try my best to send you back to your wife."

"In vitro. In glass. IVF?"

"Yes. It's what we do in the future anyway. Copulation is too hit-and-miss. Old hat."

"Heavens."

"Must go." Martin held out his hand and Derek took it.

"It's a deal then? If I get India pregnant, by any means, you'll send me back to my family?"

Martin nodded. "We're shaking on it."

"Okay, you're on. Good luck."

"And to you too, my friend". Martin faded slowly. Then he was gone.

Derek knew this hadn't been a dream. It really happened, and he was now in possession of all the facts. Then one thought occurred to him. If his sperm impregnated India, but then later things changed and he was never there, didn't that mean the children—because she was sure to have twins—were no longer in existence? Martin didn't seem to think so.

Derek's brain was trying to cope with these complex issues, and he was beginning to tire. It was already mid-afternoon but he'd start driving to Maleny. Pushing himself up from the seat, he braced for the shot of pain this movement would normally cause. No pain. He grinned and whistled his way back to the vehicle.

It wasn't until he was east of Roma that he realised what his request of Martin should really have been: not only to be sent back to 12th May 2013, but a bit earlier, even a week before the virus struck, and with full memory of all that had happened.

Derek became excited at the prospect——he could feign illness and take time off work. Yes! He'd help the kids with their homework and have dinner ready for Sophie when she came home each night. He'd talk to his wife the whole time they had left together, telling her how much she meant to him—how he loved her and depended on her and admired her.

He'd massage her tight shoulders and sore feet. When she tried to meditate, he would sit on the floor with her and do the same.

When the kids were in school and Sophie was at work, he'd drive somewhere beautiful and watch the passing parade of nature. Life would be all the more precious and wonderful for knowing that he only had a short time left to live it.

And then, on the last night, he'd let the kids stay up a little longer. He'd sit with one on each side of him and they'd look at some of their favourite books. He'd wait until they began yawning before taking them to bed and kissing them goodnight. There would be extra hugs, and he'd make sure they knew how much he loved them. Later, after they had settled down for the night, he'd slip back to their rooms and watch them sleep.

He'd then make a platter of cheeses, his and Sophie's

favourites, and serve them along with some fine wine. He and Sophie would sit and listen to music, talking softly. When they went to bed, they'd make love, or perhaps not. In any case, they would lie very close to each other. As they fell asleep, he'd make sure he was spooned into Sophie's back. He would smell her hair and press his body along the length of hers.

Would he be able to fall asleep, knowing what was coming? He thought he could. Perhaps he'd have some sleeping pills on hand, potent ones so that if sleep eluded him, he could take care of it without disturbing Sophie.

There was one thing he knew for sure. As he eventually slid into unconsciousness it would be with a smile, knowing that he was exactly where he belonged.

Part 2

CHAPTER ELEVEN

A currawong, sitting on the branch of a banksia tree outside Meg's window, woke her with its carolling. Meg smiled at the music and rolled onto her stomach, spreading her limbs across the bed.

The community had voted for a holiday, and Meg felt luxury in being able to lie in for longer. She let her mind drift over any outstanding issues, but then pushed them away again.

Her body felt good, and she was confident it looked attractive. She'd caught George watching her several times, and knew the relationship between him and Heather hadn't been good for a few months. Heather was pregnant again— her third pregnancy in four years—and it seemed she was carrying twins yet again. It was hoped that the new babies would help heal the loss of Prue, who had died in her sleep six months earlier. There were two single women in the community—herself and India. The other girl was pregnant—the story being that John impregnated her just before he lost his life in a snake attack. This didn't quite fit with what was happening around that time, but everyone just decided to shrug and accept it. To do otherwise would mean looking narrowly at Luke and George and wondering if one of them was responsible. India herself seemed puzzled by the pregnancy. It hadn't been her intention to have any more children, but stranger things had happened.

And Connie—brave girl—was also pregnant again. Four women and three pregnancies. That's why Meg felt so free in her body, so good and tight. No childbirth for her in this strange new world. She knew she should reproduce—for the good of the future population of humans—but was plain scared. She had, after all, nearly died in her last attempt at childbirth in May 2013, just as all the people of the world died.

Then there was the question of who would be the father. India had suggested, at a meeting held one night over dinner, that they use George or Luke's sperm and a process of in-vitro fertilisation. Meg wouldn't agree. There were enough pregnancies anyway, to her way of thinking.

Luke and Connie had lost a child too, the night after George and Heather's Prue died. For a long time the adults had taken turns to watch over the children as they slept. India and Meg had pored over medical books trying to find a cause, but were at a loss. They concluded that it could have been sudden infant death syndrome, but two in two nights? Meg had her own opinion, which she kept to herself. The deaths had the same feel as the bushfire, cyclone, and snake attack, like a malevolent force was trying to kill them all off.

Two things were preventing Meg from being truly happy and carefree on this holiday when the whole day would be hers, and these two things always clouded Meg's consciousness. She had a driving need to find out what happened to everyone on May 13th 2013, and she also needed to know who the odd men were who sometimes arrived in a helicopter to give them medical checks. She figured they would arrive again soon, now there were so many pregnant women.

She sat up in bed and stretched. The view from the mezzanine level of her house took in the dam and the wooden jetty that she often sat on to sip her coffee in the mornings. She could see it was going to be a stunning day.

It was chilly, though. She lay back down and covered herself with blankets. Her mind wandered, and she realised she was dozing off again. She curled into a warm ball and began breathing deeply.

"Geez, Heather. It's not that bad." George was

reaching out to her, trying to calm her as a man would with a wild horse. "For God's sake woman—lighten up." As soon as the words flew from his mouth, he knew he'd made a mistake. The look on his face said it all—he wished he could suck those words back into his throat.

"Lighten up? Lighten up?" Heather's voice kept rising. "How dare you say that? You just have no idea of how much work I do around here! I work from early in the morning to late at night. What do you do? You disappear outside after breakfast and work on 'projects'. You come in late in the day and have dinner. You get on the scotch and watch DVDs. That's your day."

"I work hard, I'll have you know!"

"Work hard? You don't even know the meaning of the words! I work from sun-up to ten o'clock at night. And I'm pregnant."

"Connie seems to cope okay."

"Look at how often Luke jumps in to help her—without even being asked. You've never done that. Not once."

Connie and Meg were working in the kitchen and could hear every word clearly. They waited for George's response. Wisely he appeared to have fallen silent. Then he spoke again. "You're just a whingeing, whining pain-in-the-arse."

Meg groaned. Things were just about to get a whole lot worse.

"Okay then, George. You looked good when you appeared to be the only man left in the world, but I've discovered you are no bargain. You might be the father of these babies I'm carrying, but that doesn't mean I have to put up with you anymore. We're done." She was talking so fast she was breathless. "What's more, as a member of this community, I'm going to put it to the group that the division of work is unfair and that you need to help out around here more."

"Bullshit!"

"Meg! Meg!"

"I'm just in the kitchen, Heather."

"Can you come in here for a moment?"

Meg walked into the living room. "Here I am."

"I'd like a review of everybody's jobs and the time they spend on them. I don't think it's fair at the moment."

"Yes, you could be right."

"We should call a meeting."

"Hmm. Perhaps we should get everyone to list their tasks first. And how long each one takes."

"Yes, great idea—as long as everybody answers

honestly." Heather glared at George.

"If you two do yours, then I'll get the others to do theirs later today. Tonight might be a bit too soon for the meeting, because I'll need to go through them all. How about tomorrow night?" Meg was keen to let emotions calm down first.

"Oh, all right. Also, George needs another place to sleep."

"Oh?" Meg raised an eyebrow at George. He shrugged.

"Yeah. As of tonight."

"Okay."

Meg could see George's chest rising and knew he was about to explode. "Bloody women! Can't you just leave a man in peace?" His hands were clenching and unclenching. "You can do up all the rosters you want, but don't think I'm going to do any bloody women's work! I'm not a bloody **sheila!**" He turned on his heel and walked out, slamming the door behind him.

Heather didn't look like she'd won an argument. As George left the house, she appeared to deflate. She sat heavily on the sofa and began weeping softly. Meg sat next to her.

"It's an age thing Heather. Some men of that generation just expect the women to do what you're doing without complaint."

"I need a younger man then."

Meg laughed. "I don't know where you're going to get one of those."

The handwritten pages were spread around Meg on the bed. She yawned and picked up the next one. It was India's. The writing was small and precise and covered four A4 sheets. India had listed the projects she was working on and had also indicated the progress and expected completion date of each.

Meg laid the pages down and rested her head on the pillow. Here was another person who shied away from housework. India would disappear into the small shed, and stay in there all day. She was remote from her children.

Meg liked India, and had from the first time she saw her struggling up the driveway with John and the twins, explaining how dreams had led them to the Maleny house. They were all in precarious health, and it had taken some time to help them recover. It turned out that the two adults were both scientists who had met quite some time after the events of May 2013. John was an expert in ecology and sustainability, while India's field was genetics.

John had been a soft man, in looks and personality. India's loyalty and commitment to him had been strong— almost fierce—and she received the same in return. She wasn't a woman to pitch in and help with domestic duties, which set her apart from Heather and Connie, but Meg understood her in some organic way. Meg could also see the value to the community in India's knowledge, and knew she could help them all by performing various tests and experiments in her shed. Meg and India had raided computer stores and laboratories so that India was well equipped to do her work.

Meg remembered the other woman's happiness when she finally had a working laboratory. India could be found at most times of the day in the small shed, leaning over something on a bench, a smile on her elfin face.

But then John had died in the act of saving the children from snakes. India confessed to Meg that he had been the only man she'd ever had a long-term relationship with and was heartbroken. She became ghost-like, emerging from her shed from time to time with a pale face, her eyes dark and huge and shadowed.

This was really the only time that Meg had seen any emotion from India, who was one of those unflappable people who were at their best in an emergency. This cool personality was worrying when it came to her children. She seemed to often forget they even existed. Connie and Heather were the ones who gave Peter and Marie the love they needed.

Now she was pregnant again, and it was unlikely that she'd be close to these children either.

Meg tapped a pencil against her teeth. Perhaps India should be taking on her fair share of the household chores, just like George. It would help her to be more social and have increased contact with Peter and Marie.

A thought struck Meg and she laughed. Peter and Marie? Marie and Pierre Curie? Had India and John named their children after the scientists who discovered radium? She realised that was very likely.

The only job sheet missing was her own. She spent a lot of time outdoors in the vegetable patch and orchard. She also was the one to plan projects and discuss them with George, and helping him physically when needed. At the end of each day, she'd also help the women with meal preparation and clearing up. She swiftly noted these details on a sheet of paper. Tomorrow night's meeting would be interesting.

The last task was the most pleasurable. She opened her journal and made detailed notes of the daily events. This always helped to clear her mind for a good night of sleep.

"I don't care. I refuse to do women's work!" George's face was beetroot-like and he was breathing deeply.

"For heaven's sake, George. Calm down. You'll blow a gasket."

George glared at Heather who pointedly turned from him.

Meg tapped her pen on the table top. "You two—this is not a kindergarten. Don't use this as an excuse to keep your petty arguments going. We will find a solution that is workable for everyone."

India had already agreed to spend more time on helping with domestic duties. George needed more jobs, but none that threatened his masculinity.

"Okay, here's a suggestion, George. You can take on the orchard and vegetable patch. What do you think?"

Heather snorted. "Everything will be dead in no time."

"Enough Heather! I was talking to George. Well, what do you think?"

"Suits me fine. My father was a market gardener."

"There—a solution and it wasn't too hard." Meg smiled.

"In fact, I almost suggested taking over the vegetable patch and orchard a few times, but I thought it was a pet project of yours."

"Yeah—to a point. But I've got them to a good stage now. I'm happy for someone else to take them over." Meg looked at the rosters. "Okay, Heather and Connie. How can India and I best help out?"

The discussion went on for another half an hour or so. George was looking bored and rose up to refill his glass of scotch. Luke watched him with a frown.

"Okay, we have our roster. It makes sense that I'm the one to do the domestic jobs that require lifting, as I'm the only non-pregnant female. Heather is still the primary child-carer, while Connie is the caterer. I'm happy to do laundry, bed-making and also go finding the things that need to be sourced from grocery-stores. We're having to expand our searches now." Everyone nodded. "George, it would really help if you checked the list before you go to get building materials. You could also be getting things needed in the household." George nodded. Apparently that didn't threaten his fragile male ego. "India, you're the backup child-care provider, along with Connie. I know it's a strain on Heather to be looking after the children so much."

"Sure. I'm okay with that."

"I reckon you could be teaching the older ones a bit of mathematics and science, too."

"Already?"

"Yeah. It would be fun. Where rain comes from. How fish breathe. You know, really basic stuff. They'd love it."

India smiled. "Yeah, I see. I'll do that."

"Now for Luke." Meg turned to him. "You've been doing a great job with the animals and birds. You also help George with many heavy tasks. On top of that, I notice how much you do to help Connie. No extra chores for you, and I reckon we should just give you a pat on the back for being such a help." Meg applauded and the others joined in.

"Any other issues?"

Heather raised her hand. "I'm a bit worried about dental care."

"What specifically?"

"We don't have access to a dentist. Lack of dental care can have really bad health side-effects. I wonder if one of us should try to learn a bit of dentistry."

"Good point. Anybody game?"

Silence fell over the group. Everybody looked at everybody else. Finally India raised her hand.

"I guess I could give it a go."

"What a gem you are, India. Thanks for that. Let's call it a night now."

George moved over to his customary DVD-watching chair and poured another scotch. Heather looked at him with distaste and went to check on the children. Connie went into the kitchen and began boiling the kettle, with Luke at her heels.

India went to a cupboard and produced a backgammon board. She raised an eyebrow at Meg who smiled in delight. A bit of recreation was most welcome.

CHAPTER TWELVE

Thwock, thwock, thwock.

The sound of the helicopter no longer caused excitement in the adults. They simply downed their respective tools with resignation, and went to the living room to await their tests.

The pregnant women were first in line, each writing comments about the state of their health on scraps of paper, which they handed to the strange, identical men whom Meg had once nicknamed Bill and Ben. Both of these men wore black suits, white shirts, and skinny black ties. They had brown eyes and swarthy skin. Both walked with strange, loose gaits, as though they were still learning the basics of physical movement. Neither one talked, and hadn't done at any time in the two-and-a-half years they had been visiting.

Equipment was unpacked, and the man with the chipped tooth, who the group had decided was Ben, motioned to Connie. Blood pressure, blood test and urine sample were all taken. Heather was next and then India. Each was handed a note to start drinking a litre of water. All three went into the kitchen to comply.

Meg was next. She handed a note to Bill. It read, "We're concerned about dental health." Bill pocketed the note with the ones from the other three women. Meg's tests were completed quickly, and then Ben grabbed her left arm to ensure the implant was still in place—Meg had removed two previously. This one was still there.

George and Luke were examined while Heather lined up the children. Bill had a jar of jelly beans ready, and unsmilingly handed one to each child after their examinations. Thomas, Luke and Connie's boy, was inclined to be cheeky. He popped the jelly bean into his mouth quickly and held out his hand for another. Bill frowned and didn't seem to know how to react. He reached into the jar for another bean and gave it to the child, who crowed in delight.

Ben was fiddling with the ultrasound machine, which he'd set up near the sofa. Connie approached and lay on her back. While Ben ran the scanner over Connie's swollen belly, Meg peered over Ben's shoulder at the screen.

This procedure was repeated for the other two pregnant women.

Finally, there was nothing left to do, and the men began packing up. Samples were placed in purpose-built cases. Data was entered into a compact machine, and Meg guessed it was transmitted immediately to some unknown person or persons.

The chickens became unsettled as the helicopter began its pre-flight rotor rotations. Meg knew there wouldn't be many eggs the next day. The aircraft rose unsteadily and hovered for a moment before gaining altitude. The men weren't good pilots and often had startled looks on their faces as they flew away.

"Well, that's that then!" Meg sighed and pulled her rubber gloves back on. "Don't I love cleaning bathrooms!"

India chuckled as they all went their different ways.

"Okay, so we just have to lift this beam. It's a load-bearing one, so quite heavy. Are you sure you're up for this Meg?"

"I'm okay, George. Luke will take a lot of the weight at his end."

"You'll let me know if you can't handle it, won't you?"

"Yup. Let's do this."

The heavy piece of timber was placed into a position that satisfied George. Luke wiped his hands on a rag and wandered away.

"How come you're working on your place at this time

of day, anyway? I thought you promised that you'd only work on your house when all your other work was finished."

George looked down and kicked at a tuft of grass. "Um, yeah. Sorry. I was just worried about that beam. Thought you two might prefer to do it in daytime."

"I see. I'd hate to think the vegetables—"

"Nup. Promise. Cross my heart. I'm just heading there now."

George had decided to build a small house of his own since Heather had kicked him out of their bed. The good thing about this was that George mostly worked on building it in the early evening, which meant he was drinking less.

"I'll walk over to the veggie patch with you. I want to ask you a few things."

"You're unhappy with what I'm doing?" His face was a picture of disappointment.

"No—heavens, don't get me wrong! I'm very happy." They were approaching the enclosure. "In fact I wanted to ask you how you got the tomatoes looking so healthy. And the lettuces!"

"Ah, I see. You want to steal my secrets!" His eyes were twinkling.

Meg laughed. "Only if you want to share them with me."

"I'll tell you, but it will cost you." He took a step closer.

Meg sighed. "Oh, yeah? Cost me what?"

"You know."

"How many times do I have to tell you George—I'm not interested. Don't take it personally."

"C'mon. Tell me what you don't like about me. I'll change."

"Nothing specifically about you. I just don't want a relationship."

"Ha! Well, there you have it. We don't have to have a relationship. Just some fun."

"No. No. No."

George sighed. "It's just been so long."

"Heather only finished with you a couple of months ago."

"Ten weeks, and things had been a bit quiet in the bedroom a long time before that, if you get my drift."

"Oh, I see."

"My grandfather was Italian, you know."

"So?"

"We Italian guys are great in the sack. I could do things to you—"

"I don't think so."

"Look!" He pointed to his groin, which was swollen

and straining against his track pants.

"Hmm. Yes. Very nice. You can be proud of it. I'm sure you're a stud."

George seemed to miss the irony in her voice. "I used to make Heather happy, keep her satisfied."

"I'm sure you did, and what's more, I think you could put things back to right with her."

"Really?"

"Yeah. The twins are due very soon. Be supportive. Help her. Shave every day. Stay off the booze."

George raised his eyebrows. "Do you think so?"

"Yup. You might have to be a bit patient, though. Don't be the first to make the move. Just be friendly and helpful. She might just come 'round—after the babies are born and she recovers."

"Gawd. That long?"

"Yes, George. Patience."

"But in the meantime—"

"What?"

"You and I. We could just..."

"No, no, NO."

But as she walked away, feigning anger, she could feel the effect the man was having on her. He wasn't the type she would normally find attractive, but he had aroused her and he was *there*.

Images began flashing through her mind. They were erotic and electric. She tried to banish them.

As Meg rounded the corner of the house she came across the Border collie they had saved as a puppy and raised as a guard dog. It was sitting with its legs open, licking its genitals. A bright red penis, erect and pointed, was waving at her. She groaned and clapped her hands until the dog ran toward Luke and the cows.

What was this, she thought. A conspiracy?

"You and George looked friendly out there." Heather was on the sofa, with her feet on the coffee table. Her hands were resting on her belly, which was straining like an overripe melon.

Meg smiled. "Yes, we were talking about the great job he's doing. The lettuces and tomatoes are amazing. Had I known his father had been a market gardener—"

"I don't mean that."

"What?"

"You and him."

Meg was just about to suggest that hearing the possibility from George was bad enough, without Heather suggesting it as well, when she realised what a bad idea that would be.

"There's no such thing as him and me."

Heather's eyes narrowed. "Are you sure?"

"Let me tell you two things, Heather. You kicked George out, so he's available. If I did want to take him on, I wouldn't need your permission. The fact is that I'm just not interested at the moment."

"But you might be in the future?"

Meg bit her lip. Perhaps a bit of jealousy would help to bring about a reconciliation. "Dunno. Might do."

"He's straightened himself out a bit—even lost weight since he started building the house."

"Yeah, I noticed. He's almost a new man."

"India might get interested in him too, you know."

"Maybe. There's such a shortage of men."

Heather patted her belly. "These babies had better come soon. I need to start looking good again."

"So, you must be around thirty-six weeks now."

"Yeah, not sure, but around that."

"Don't wish for them too soon."

"Do you realise I must've gotten pregnant nearly straight after having Prue and Candace?" Heather's face changed when she spoke about her dead daughter. Shadows appeared, and she looked drawn.

"I thought breast-feeding protected you from that."

"Not in this new world of ours. We're just baby factories, we women."

Meg snorted. "Yeah, that's one way of putting it. Contraception next?"

"Won't need it if George and I stay apart."

"Oh, I don't think you'll be apart for long."

"Maybe not."

The two women smiled at each other.

"Anyway, when it comes to George, I think you're the woman for him."

"Really?"

"Yup. Really. You two were just made for each other. Stop fretting now. Men don't like their women too possessive."

The babies were born two days later. A sober and clean-shaven George stood by Heather's side and wiped her forehead with a cool cloth, holding water to her lips whenever he was asked.

Meg had originally been very concerned when she realised that the labour was happening early—around four weeks premature—but she needn't have worried. She and India worked side by side, one delivering and one checking the babies as they emerged, and were satisfied that the newborns were as healthy as could be expected.

For their third set of twins, George and Heather were blessed with a boy and a girl. "The boy will be named George junior," said Heather firmly, smiling at the man by her side. "And maybe you should make that house a little bit bigger."

"Really?" George's grin lit the room.

"Yes. I think so."

George bowed. "Consider it done, my beautiful lady."

Meg turned away and busied herself with the new baby girl. As she lifted the squirming bundle to kiss its cheek, she whispered, "Maybe your mother and father aren't so silly after all." India heard and smiled.

CHAPTER THIRTEEN

"C'mon sleepyhead. Open the door!" Meg banged on the door of the caravan a second time. She felt the van rock as India's feet touched the floor, and with each footstep. A hinge squealed as the door opened.

"What's wrong?" Her face looked bare without the customary black-framed glasses.

"Nothing. It's a stunning winter's day. Blue skies and no wind. Don't you love Queensland?"

India frowned. "You woke me for this—a weather report?" She turned and walked back towards her bed. "Shut the door after you. It's cold."

"No, it's gorgeous."

"That's because you're a southerner. We Queenslanders know a cold morning when we feel one." India snuggled back under the blankets.

"Aw, c'mon. I have to go to Maroochydore for some things. Thought you might want to come along."

"Why?"

"To help me."

"Do what?"

"Oh, I need your opinion and you could help lift things."

"Not with this belly, I can't."

"Won't be anything heavy, just bulky."

"I dunno. How long will this take?"

"Just a few hours."

"And you need my help?"

"Yes. Please?"

"Okay." India swung her legs out of bed again. "I'll just have a shower."

"No need. We can go for a swim."

"Swim? Jeez, Meg. You're crazy. We'd freeze!"

"Just a quick paddle."

India was shaking her head as she reached for her usual uniform of jeans and t-shirt. A woollen jumper was hauled over her head.

Meg noted India's bulging abdomen with interest. If it was true that John impregnated her just before he died from snakebites, then the woman would be full-term already. She was certainly a long way from that stage. Who was the father, then?

As India began brushing her teeth, Meg began

planning. "I'll go and check with Connie, she's sure to have a list of things needed. See you in five?"

"Sure."

Meg crossed the lawn, her feet squashing ice on the grass, making a crunching sound. She smiled and looked skyward. The air was particularly clear, and there wasn't one cloud to mar the soaring blue skies. It was one of those days that made her want to hold her arms wide and turn in loose circles. She laughed and did just that.

Maisie came toddling out of the house, giggling. She opened her arms and began spinning quickly. When she stopped, Meg could see that the girl's eyes kept moving and Maisie began swaying. Her legs gave way and she sat with a thud. "Funny!" She giggled and clambered up to begin spinning again.

"What are you two up to?" Connie had been watching them with a smile.

"Celebrating a perfect day."

Connie took a step forward so she could see past the verandah overhang. "Oh, yes. Lovely."

"India and I are going to Maroochydore for supplies. Want anything?"

"Oh lots. I'll grab the list." She disappeared into the darkness and returned with a piece of paper. "These are the food items. But could you see if you can get some hairdressing things?"

"Like...?"

"New scissors—ours are blunt and rusty. New clippers for the boys' hair. More brushes and combs?"

"Sure."

"Oh, and one of those capes. You know—that hairdressers use..."

"Got it. Is that it?"

"Um. Oh, we're having rabbit casserole tonight."

"The first farmed bunny?"

Connie nodded.

"That'll be interesting."

"Yes, but George said that the casserole had to have red wine in it." Connie frowned.

"Well, for once I agree with George on an alcohol issue. Only the flavour is left—the actual alcohol will cook out of it."

"Oh, okay then."

"I'll just get one of those wine casks. Quality won't matter. That way you'll have some more for the next casserole."

"Good idea."

"What else?"

Connie looked at her list for a few seconds, then shook her head. Meg walked past her to the kitchen and took two bananas and two mandarins from the bowl on the bench. As she strode away, she waved.

By the time she got to the car, India was sitting in the passenger seat.

"We won't be more than the few hours you said? I've got lots to do."

Meg shook her head. "Relax. Just pretend we're playing truant." She rolled through the pot-holes carefully, mindful of India's condition.

"I guess it'll be a race between you and Connie for the next round of childbirth."

India rolled her eyes. "I guess so, although Connie looks a lot more advanced than me."

"Yes, she does." Meg looked at the other woman sideways, but India made no more comments on the subject.

They chattered about inconsequential matters for some time, until Maroochydore came into view.

"We've got four places to go—then we'll hit the beach. You'll be hot by then."

India just shook her head.

"There we go. All done."

India looked into the back of the small sedan and frowned. "You really didn't need my help. I guess you just wanted company."

Meg laughed. "I'll tell you a secret. It's my birthday."

"Oh, wow. Happy birthday! How old?"

"Forty."

"Gee, a milestone birthday, too. Congratulations!"

"Thanks."

"You keep track of the dates, don't you? So you'd know when it's a special day."

"I do. When's yours? Birthday?"

"September the sixth."

"Virgo."

"Yeah, so what's the date today?"

"June twenty-eighth."

"No wonder you want to swim in the sea. You're a crab!"

Meg laughed gaily. "Exactly".

"Well, I'm honoured that you picked me to spend your special day with."

"You're a clear choice. Couldn't be George, he'd be after me like a dog on heat."

India chuckled. "And I guess Luke wouldn't be appropriate. There's Connie and Heather."

"Hmm. But, you know, I don't feel like I have any common ground with them. They're just so bogged down with motherhood and home duties."

"Yeah, I know what you mean. I certainly don't share any interest with those two."

"And there's something else I just realised—just now—that they remind me of how I was during my marriage. I didn't like myself much then. Later I began a career..." She swung into a parking lot at the beach. "But don't get me wrong. I admire those two, the way they cope with all of that. I'm just past it."

"And I was never there to start with. But, you know, Heather might surprise you."

"How?"

"Well, we got talking once. She's got an interesting story about the man she was in love with, back in 2013."

"Really? In what way was it interesting?"

"I didn't get the full story. You should ask her yourself."

"Okay, I will, but there never seems to be time." Meg leapt out and moved to the back of the vehicle. As the hatch opened, she began organising their beach outing. "I have a chair and towel for each of us. We can sit in the shade under the overhang of that big tree if you want."

India opened her door and braced herself for the cold. She was pleasantly surprised, however. The air was still and warm.

They moved down to the sand, and Meg opened a chair out for India, being careful that all the catches were in place before setting it down. Then she gazed out to the gentle surf.

"Damn!"

"What?"

"I forgot my swimsuit." She looked across the road to a row of shops, hoping to see swimwear in the window.

"Nobody's going to see you, Meg."

"You don't mind?"

"Of course not."

Meg was wearing a dress and cardigan. Both of these were dealt with quickly, and she ran to the edge of the water. She splashed into the shallows, gasping as the water hit her midriff. She dived under a small wave and then began swimming with an easy freestyle stroke.

Gasping for breath, she trod water as she looked back toward the beach. India's chair was empty.

Meg was astonished when the other woman's head rose up beside her. "Couldn't let you have all the fun, could I?"

They bobbed in the waves for a few minutes. India

179

began shivering and struck back to shore. Meg swam for another few minutes before she also decided to head back to the beach.

India had already dressed again, and Meg did the same. They sat in their chairs, contemplating the endless stretch of water before them.

"I wonder what it would feel like..."

"What?"

"Drowning. They say it's peaceful."

Meg looked at the other woman closely.

"No, I'm not suicidal or anything. I just wondered."

"That's okay then."

"It would solve one problem though."

"What?" Meg noticed an almost invisible hole in the side of India's nose, evidence of a past piercing.

"Drowning. It would solve the dilemma about where I belong."

"What do you mean?"

"It's hard to describe, but I feel like I shouldn't be here. Shouldn't still be alive. Not like a guilt thing or anything like that. It's just that I don't belong here. Do you know what I mean?"

"Who did you lose?"

"Oh, no-one really. As I said, it isn't a guilt thing. I

don't feel like I miss anyone so much that I should have died with them or anything. It's just a sense that it's just not right that I'm here."

"Not right?"

"I'm not supposed to be here. I don't belong."

Meg considered this for a moment and realised that she'd felt the same from time to time, especially back when it all first happened.

"Actually, yeah. I think I know what you mean."

India turned to her quickly. "You do?"

"Yes, I've felt that way sometimes."

They sat quietly for a few moments, lost in their own thoughts.

India chuckled. "We could turn this into a sort of metaphysical debate."

"A what?"

"Metaphysical debate—you know—philosophy."

"No, I don't know."

"Metaphysics tries to answer the big questions, like the fundamental nature of being."

"Good heavens."

"Existence, cause and effect, time..."

"Wow. All the big questions indeed."

"It would be interesting right now, given our

circumstances in this strange new world of ours."

"So many questions to be answered!"

"But sadly we don't have a clue."

"I mean, why are we here, really?"

"Yes, that's a good one."

"You take Luke and Connie. They never seem to question it. They seem to have accepted that this is their world now."

"I've noticed that." India pointed to a seagull that only had one leg. Meg smiled and nodded.

"They just bob along, having babies and doing hard work, almost as though that's what they're *meant* to be doing."

"True."

"But I don't feel that way and it seems you don't either."

"Exactly. John shared my feelings, too."

Meg went to the car and returned with the fruit.

India reached for it eagerly. "Brilliant! Thanks, Meg."

They peeled their mandarins in silence, the smell of the sweet fruit making their mouths fill with saliva. India popped a segment into her mouth and began talking again. "Socrates and Plato were big into the subject."

"Metaphysics? The name sounds like a science more than a philosophy. So it's not a new thing if those two were into it."

India laughed. "Indeed not. Man first began questioning these things at the beginning of time—well the beginning of time as far as humans were concerned. Plato's student, Aristotle, was also involved in some of the early work on the subject."

"So have you debated metaphysics yourself?"

"Oh, in coffee shops as a student."

A slight breeze blew in to shore, and both women shivered slightly. Meg stood. "One more quick swim. Coming?"

India huddled into the chair, her arms crossed and shoulders hunched. "No, I'll leave that to you."

As Meg ran down to the water's edge, she pondered India's question about drowning, wondering how it would feel.

"Oh, no!"

"What?"

Meg tapped the dashboard display. "Oil warning light."

"Oh? What does that mean?"

"It means trouble."

"Will we make it home?"

"I'll try, but I don't like our chances."

Meg had a flashback. She was driving on a dirt road, her father beside her, and he was issuing instructions. "And if that oil light comes on, girlie, you're in deep shit. It means the engine ain't got enough oil pressure to protect itself. If you don't want to seize the whole show up—and let me tell you, you don't—you just have to stop the bloody car. Straight away." Meg sighed.

"Why are you sighing?"

"Just remembering what Dad said. I think we're in trouble, but I'm going to keep driving anyway."

Their distance to home wasn't greatly decreased before the car's engine cut out.

"There it is then." Meg sighed again. She located the bonnet release and pulled it savagely. Soon she had the hood up and was looking into the engine bay. "Yep. It's a motor alright, but I think it's dead."

"Maybe it just has to cool down or something."

"Not likely. At least it stopped in the shade."

The road they were on was sealed, and they'd stopped under some eucalyptus trees. The shade was speckled, and the women could still feel the heat from the road and the sun. Meg looked around. There weren't any houses within sight, but she figured there must be some set back from the road.

"Funny that I was complaining about the cold this

morning." India pulled the jumper off over her head.

"Yes..." Meg wasn't really listening. She was considering their situation. "I guess they'll come for us eventually. They knew where we were going."

"For sure."

"I wonder how long—"

"Eventually. When it gets dark I guess." India looked around the car. "Don't suppose we have water?"

"Um, don't know." Meg swung around to look in the back. "Must be something in the car here."

"Don't worry yet."

"I can go and get some if we need it."

"Not yet."

India opened her door. Bees hummed in the nearby bushes. The sky was still cloudless.

Meg looked at India. "How much water did you have before you left home this morning?"

"One glass. Small."

"I'd better go and get you some."

"Why don't you try the car again?"

"It won't work."

"Try anyway."

Meg turned the key in the ignition. Nothing.

"Ah, well. Worth a try."

"I'd better go for water then."

"I'll come with you."

"No, I'll be quicker by myself."

"I'm only pregnant. Not sick."

"Still, I'd rather go alone."

The first driveway Meg came to was overgrown, but she was able to pick her way over the weeds, including high thistles, and walk up toward the house.

A depressing sight greeted her. Some livestock that were being held in a small enclosure had died, probably of starvation, and their bones were now bleached by the sun.

She discovered the house was unlocked and quickly moved into the cool kitchen. The tap had seized and her attempts to free it just hurt her hand. She found a tea-towel and used it for protection. Finally the handle moved, but the water was discoloured and smelled bad.

She opened the pantry and peered into its depths, hoping to find some bottled water or any drinkable fluids. There was nothing.

At the next farmhouse, she found the same scenario. Foul water and nothing else to drink.

Walking back to the car, she saw India step from the car to greet her. "No luck?"

"Nope. I'll try in the other direction."

"The shade's disappearing."

"There's still some under that other tree. Take a chair."

"Oh, yeah. Great."

Meg trudged along the hot road, cursing her lack of foresight. A set of gates appeared on her left—modern looking. Her spirits lifted.

This property appeared to be a horse stud or spelling yard. Saddles and blankets, degraded by weather, hung over fence-railing. There were no animal carcases, in the vicinity of the house at least.

As she approached the building, she noted how secure it looked, as though it had been particularly well locked-up before May 2013. She tried opening the front entry, but it was a solidly constructed security door and wouldn't budge. All the windows had modern shutters which didn't allow access, or even the ability to smash the glass. Meg realised that all the heavy tools she used for accessing shops were back home in the four-wheel-drive.

As she turned to her left, she noticed that this farm stood at the edge of a national park. No more houses.

Taps! There had to be taps in the stables. She ran into one of the outbuildings and disconnected a hose from one of the brass fittings. She turned the handle of the tap, but nothing happened. Not even a drop.

How could that be? There was always plenty of rain in the region. How could the tanks be dry? Unless this farm was on town water. Meg groaned. She searched for tanks with growing desperation but didn't find any.

The walk back to the car seemed ten times longer than it should have been. India had placed the two chairs under a tree. As she saw Meg's empty hands she smiled.

"You tried your best."

"It's just stupid."

"It won't really hurt us to go without water for a few more hours."

"But you will have been without it all day. You need it."

"I'll be fine."

Meg searched the car for anything remotely drinkable. All she found was the cask of rough red wine for the rabbit casserole. She held it up.

"Diuretic. Bad idea."

"I'm still going to have a mouthful—just to wet my mouth. It was pretty hot and dry walking out there."

She looked for something to pour it into but came up empty-handed. "I'll have to drink it straight out of the cask."

"I'll help. Sit down."

India opened the carton where the tap was and extended it out. "Head back."

She pressed the top of the tap gently until some drops appeared. She pressed harder and there was a gush of wine. "Oops."

Meg waved her hands and began coughing. Then the laughter started and wine began dribbling down her chin. "Well, that certainly washed my mouth out!"

She replaced the cask in the car and saw the hairdressing supplies. Grinning, she opened out the cape and flicked it like a matador. "Haircut, ma'am?"

"Yes, thank you!"

Meg found the comb and was soon running it through India's cropped, black hair.

"You won't need much trimmed off."

"Just a wee tidy-up."

Meg took her time, trying to make sure she was cutting each section to the same length as those before it.

"It would help if your hair was wet."

"Ha! Then we'd need water!"

Meg groaned. "Wine?"

They laughed. Time ticked by and all that could be heard was the snipping of hair and calling of birds.

"All done."

"Your turn."

"Oh, okay. I'll just have another sip of that wine. Thirsty work."

She sat and put her head back, opening her mouth like a baby bird. India tried to control the volume of wine being dispensed, but it still came in a rush. Meg gasped for breath. "I don't know which is worse, the bad wine or the choking on it!"

India was surveying Meg's hair critically. The tight curls looked like a challenge. She bit her lip and pulled a few strands straight before chopping them quickly. Then she went to the next section. After a few more minutes she stood back and surveyed her handiwork. "Hmm. Needs some evening up."

She snipped worriedly for a few more minutes and then inspected the result. "Nope. I'm just making it worse. I should leave it to Connie. She's a natural at cutting hair."

India returned the implements to the car and sat down next to Meg. She began whistling, and a bird replied. Both women laughed.

The sun was hanging low, the west turning a beautiful shade of burned orange. The evening star began shining. The world was very still.

Meg sensed a special quietness in India. She looked and

found that the other woman had fallen asleep. She smiled and reached for the wine cask. An attempt to pour it in to her own mouth was a disaster and she could feel the wetness of wine running between her breasts. She gasped for air and coughed so loudly that India stirred.

"What was that?"

"Nothing. Go back to sleep."

"Oh, look!"

They looked at the sky in wonder. A new moon was cradling the evening star as the light faded. They gazed, stupefied by the beauty of the moment.

Meg became aware of the discomfort of having a bra soaked in red wine against her skin. She found a chamois in the glove box of the car and began patting at the spillage.

India looked on in amusement. "I think I'll have a mouthful of that wine..."

"Sure. But don't blame me for the results."

After two careful attempts by Meg, India was able to rinse her dry mouth. "Surely they'll come soon."

"They're sure to. Hey, I noticed your tattoo today. Very intricate."

India reached over to the base of her neck, where it met the top of the spine. "Do you like it?"

"Nice."

"It's a wedding ring. Celtic."

"Wedding ring?"

"Yeah."

"So?"

"Oh, it's a long story. When I was at uni a girl and I—"

"A girl?"

"Yeah. We met and, well, things progressed fairly quickly."

"A strong attraction, hey?"

"Definitely, but more than that. A bond."

"I see."

"I can be a bit funny in relationships."

"In what way?"

"Hard to explain. Intense."

"Obsessive? You seemed that way with John."

"Well, he was my first man—and there's only been two people in the whole of my life."

"John and this girl?"

"Yes. Anyway, knowing how her parents would be if they found out—"

"Really? How long ago was this?"

"Fifteen years. They were wealthy socialites—you know the type. She was their only child."

"I see."

"So I talked her into having our own little ceremony and we both got this tattoo..." She was still rubbing the spot.

"But?"

"But it didn't last. She fell into line with her parents' wishes."

"How were you when that happened?"

"Not good."

Meg nodded.

"I mean really not good. We broke up in my final year of uni. I just scraped through. Nearly threw it all in."

"You didn't seem too bad after John died."

India looked at her steadily in the near darkness. "I didn't do well, Meg."

"Oh, I'm sorry."

"That's okay. You weren't to know."

"I should have been there more for you."

India shook her head. No, I'm better off alone when I'm like that."

When Meg moved her head it seemed the rest of the world wasn't quite keeping up. "I think that wine's a bit potent."

"Probably."

"We might be more comfortable in the car now. Put the seats back."

"Sure. Let's give it a go."

They reclined the seats and India lay on her side, facing Meg. She smiled and fell asleep.

Meg lay looking at her and digesting what she'd just learned. Visions of India making love to another woman swam though her mind and she felt a jolt of arousal.

She wondered if she could do that—make love to a woman. Some people moved between the sexes easily, but not Meg. Still, the thought had possibilities.

She examined the other woman's face in the semi-darkness. India's glasses were sitting on the dashboard. Meg could see her long lashes and flushed cheeks. Her breath smelled of the mouthful of wine she'd taken. Meg wondered what it would be like to press her lips gently against India's.

Headlights flashed into the car. Meg opened her door gently, trying to be as quiet as possible. As she stood, the world around her swayed.

George stopped the four-wheel-drive and leapt out. He surveyed Meg with interest, taking in the wine-stained clothing. "Wow. Looks like you two have been having a party. Gawd, what's happened to your hair?"

Meg walked toward him and swayed. George moved quickly to support her. "Steady on."

"Got any water?"

"Um. Not that I know of." He searched the vehicle. "No, sorry."

"I had to drink wine."

"I see that. So you're tipsy and India has passed out."

"Not from alcohol. She's just tired and thirsty and pregnant."

Meg swayed again and George grabbed her. He looked into her face and brushed some hair clippings from her forehead. He smiled and put both his arms around her. Lowering himself to her height, he then put his mouth to hers, gently at first, but then rougher and more insistently.

Meg tried to push him away, but he kept a firm hold on her. He ground his pelvis into hers and she could feel his erection. He moved one hand under her dress and began feeling her. She was slippery. While manipulating her, he reached down and tugged at his track pants.

Meg was ready. She was aroused and wet and needy. It was her birthday damn it. George spun her around so that she could bend over the seat of the four-wheel-drive. He was going to enter her from behind. The thought alone made her groan.

India coughed in her sleep. This brought Meg back to reality. What was happening here? She had a sudden sense of having been manipulated, like it was a set-up. There was a memory, just the germ of a one, about being manipulated into pregnancy. "No!" she yelled forcefully. She pushed George away.

"What?"

"No. I said no."

"Too late. You can't do that to a man. Look at me!" He clutched his engorged penis and waved it at her.

"You can't take advantage of a woman who's had too much to drink through no fault of her own." She could tell her words were getting through. "That's not nice. Give me any more trouble and I'll tell Heather." His erection began to shrink.

"But you could do other things, you know. You could still—"

"For Christ sakes George. Do it yourself. But not now, we have to get India home and re-hydrated."

As they drove up to the community house, it was to the sight of Heather, Connie and Luke standing on the front verandah, waiting to see if Meg and India would return safely. There were exclamations as Meg emerged from the backseat, smiling. "Here we are, all good. George rescued us."

After getting India what she needed, Meg said goodnight and drove back a bit tipsily to her own house.

It was only when she woke the next day, refreshed and sober, that she realised how close she'd come to falling pregnant in this strange new world where it would be dangerous for her to do so.

CHAPTER FOURTEEN

Meg rolled the dice and moved her backgammon pieces swiftly. She leaned toward India and began whispering. "I'm a bit worried about Connie."

"Yeah, I know."

"What have you noticed?"

"Oedema. Tiredness. I thought we should take her blood pressure."

"Could be toxaemia like I had—years ago."

"Maybe. We could do with a visit from Bill and Ben."

"I wish there was a way to call them."

India rolled the dice and rubbed her hands together in glee. "Double sixes. Ha! You're toast."

"It's not over until the fat lady sings."

India leaned forward again. "Perhaps just light duties?"

"I was thinking bed-rest."

"Sure. Can you cook?"

Meg laughed. "In a fashion. We won't starve, but we'll miss Connie's food. Hey, Connie!"

"Yes, Meg?" The younger woman walked awkwardly into the room, wiping her hands on a tea-towel.

"We've made a decision. Bed-rest for you. Until the babies are born." Connie looked from one to another in bewilderment.

"But—who will cook?"

"We'll manage."

"Oh, I don't know..."

"Hey Luke!"

"Yeah?"

"Take Connie and put her in bed. From now on it's bed-rest until the bubs are born. Okay?"

Luke rushed into the room with round eyes. "Who'll cook?"

"For heaven's sakes, Luke—we'll manage." India nodded her head in support of Meg's words.

Luke started chewing his lip as he took Connie's arm to lead her into the bedroom. He looked like a condemned man.

As if summoned, Bill and Ben guided the helicopter unsteadily onto the property the very next morning. They moved quickly into Connie's bedroom and began taking samples and running tests. Ben entered details of Connie's vital signs into a machine. When it came to a urine sample,

Connie wasn't allowed out of bed to go to the bathroom, but had to pass urine into a bedpan and this was transferred to a bottle.

Meg was handed a note, which read SHE MUST NOT LEAVE THE BED. Bill administered an injection which made Connie fall asleep quickly.

The two men moved with as much speed as their ungainly gait would allow to the helicopter, and left immediately. It sounded to Meg as though the aircraft was being flown at full throttle.

"No doubt they've scared the chickens again."

She moved to the kitchen to see what she could possibly feed all these people for lunch.

"Open wide, George. That's a good fella."

India was leaning over the man, peering into his cavernous mouth. "Hmm. I think what this whole community needs is a lecture in dental hygiene."

Meg nodded. "We should be giving the kids daily lessons. You've taken to dentistry very well."

"Yeah, but I'm yet to do an extraction, but if George doesn't start brushing properly and flossing every day, it won't be long before he'll need some of his molars pulled."

George made a sound in his throat.

"Almost finished. I reckon there is some decay in one of your rear molars at the very least. I'll have to read up more on how to clean the tooth out and fill it."

George's eyes became round and the noises from his throat were becoming more urgent sounding.

"Well, we don't want toothache and abscesses and things, George. Very nasty. You can end up with terrible staph infections, too." She removed the instruments. "Cleaning and flossing, George. Twice a day."

George sat straight up, his face pale. "Okay. I'll start straight away."

"Here's the floss and a fresh toothbrush. Go for it."

As George almost ran out the door, India smiled at Meg. "Not a whiff of scotch on the breath, either."

"And no whiskers. A changed man indeed."

"What are we going to cook for dinner tonight?"

Meg looked at her tiredly. "Gosh, I don't know. I suppose we'd better find something quickly."

"The sun's already going down."

"How did Connie ever do that for all of us?"

"Dunno."

"How about I set up the spaghetti making machine?"

"Yeah. Fun."

"I think it takes about half an hour to make the pasta,

then there's the sauce..."

"Just a Neapolitan one—tomatoes, onion, and garlic?"

"Done!" The two women smiled at one another. "I'll set it up now."

"I'll get the veggies."

"It will be a fine feast!"

George chewed on his dinner slowly. At first he looked puzzled, then he frowned.

"So, um. What do you call this?"

Heather was chewing on a mouthful of hers, while playing with the rest in a desultory fashion.

"Fettuccine with Neapolitan sauce. Don't you like it?" Meg sat down and tasted hers. She chewed mournfully. "I see." She looked at India and the other woman shrugged her shoulders.

"We tried our best."

Heather pushed her plate away. "George's heritage is Italian, you know."

"Really? Yes, I see that now. You could probably make a mean pasta," said India.

"Yes, I could."

"That's not women's work, you know. Look at all the great chefs in the world. The greater percentage are men."

Meg was warming to the theme.

"I've always thought that chefs were really sexy, too," said India, kicking Meg under the table.

"Oh, yeah. Definitely."

George was nodding. "I suppose I could cook occasionally."

"Just until Connie's back on her feet."

Heather put her hand over George's. "What a wonderful way to support your family. Growing the produce and then making it into magnificent meals. What a man!"

Luke was the only one eating the meal. He was listening with a look of amusement.

"Well, alright. I'll give it a go tomorrow night. We'll see how it turns out."

Meg woke next morning with a sense of foreboding. She lay still and closed her eyes, trying to pick up whatever vibes were coming her way. What could it be? The answer came at once. Connie.

This thought made Meg sit upright quickly. She reached for her clothes, but then reconsidered. If anything was happening, someone from the community would have come to fetch her. Instead of dressing, she showered and ate some scrambled eggs and tomatoes.

As she washed the dishes, she gazed out over the Glasshouse Mountains. The air was very clear, so clear that she felt she could reach out and touch the unusual protuberance that stood vertically from Mt Coonowrin. She moved through the glass doors and down to the edge of the cleared section of land. The view was magnificent. She lifted her arms and breathed deeply. Whatever happened on this day couldn't take away the magic of the perfect morning.

She was having difficulty dragging herself away from the perfect scene, until a sound made her crash back to reality. It was the helicopter, and its pitch implied urgency. Then she saw a cloud of dust coming from the direction of the other house. A car. Her sense of foreboding was growing by the minute.

She ran to the driveway to meet the other vehicle. India was driving.

"Quick. Connie's in trouble." India's eyes shifted to a point over Meg's shoulder and she began frowning. "That helicopter..."

"What?" Meg turned and looked. The aircraft was above them and descending rapidly. "Jeez, they'd better be careful!" It began skewing from side to side. "What the hell is he doing?"

Both women watched open-mouthed. The helicopter

rose rapidly and then lost altitude just as quickly.

"Oh God. Meg, look—it's in trouble."

The two women watched in horrified fascination as the aircraft began spinning. It spiralled downward, until it was obscured behind trees. They heard terrible noises of mechanical chaos.

Meg got into India's car. "We'll go and see if we can save them."

"What about Connie?"

"God. Damn. Geez, I don't know. You go back to Connie and tell her I'm coming. I'll go and have a quick look and see what I can do."

"No, you go and see Connie. I'll look at what's happening with the helicopter."

"Yeah, you're right."

Meg drove her own car to the community house. As she entered, she could hear Connie's moans. Luke was by her side and as white as a sheet.

"Did I hear the helicopter? Are they coming to help?"

"Maybe. Let's just see what's going on here."

Meg took Connie's blood pressure and frowned. She lifted the sheet and spread Connie's knees apart, then swore.

"Go and grab Heather, would you Luke?"

"Where's India?"

"Doing something else urgent. I need Heather quickly."

The next few hours were a blur. In the midst of the trauma, Meg was aware of India returning in her car, but she didn't appear in the house to assist. Meg and Heather did everything possible, but the end result was one live child, one who didn't survive, and a mother close to death.

They handed the live baby to Luke and concentrated on Connie. The girl was delirious, moving in and out of consciousness. Finally she lay completely still, breathing shallowly.

"Let's leave her be for now. Luke, just sit there and keep an eye on her would you? I'll be back shortly."

Meg strode out of the house, banging the door behind her. She had needed India so desperately, but the other woman had disappeared. Where in the hell had she gone?

India's small sedan was parked outside her shed, and the back passenger door was hanging open. Meg ran past it into the shed entry where she was greeted by an extraordinary sight.

India was bent over a figure on the single bed. She had an array of equipment around her, and was moving up and down the figure, measuring and probing.

"Meg, sorry. Really sorry. I know I was needed, but this

was a case of very exceptional circumstances."

"Who is this?" Meg moved closer, looking at the figure in an attempt to get some clues.

"Bill and Ben are dead, but our friend here was also in the helicopter. So far he has survived."

"Good Lord. He looks very old!"

"That's not all. Anyway, I'm trying to stabilise him."

"What do you mean, that's not all?"

"This gentleman has some rather interesting features. I'll tell you later. How is Connie?"

"Not good."

"Babies?"

"One died."

"Jeez. I'm sorry Meg. It must've been awful. I think this guy here was coming to help her."

"I wish he could have helped."

"How serious is Connie?"

"Her blood pressure was a problem. We got the babies out as quick as we could, but she was delirious. She's settled now, and Luke is watching her."

"Are you afraid of stroke or pre-eclampsia?"

"Either. Both. I don't know. Even though I've had it myself, I still don't know quite how it works. I've just got my fingers crossed that the babies came out in time before any lasting harm was done."

"Pre-eclampsia can kill, can't it?"

"Yes."

India sighed. "I feel so bad about not being there."

"I don't think you could have changed the outcome."

"No, I suppose not."

"So this guy—"

"I need to sequence his DNA."

"Huh?"

"There's something weird here. I don't want to speculate, but I need to get some of his DNA to UQ and run a genome sequence."

"UQ? The university in Brisbane?"

"Yup. There are backup generators there."

"So you'll take some of his DNA with you and leave him here?"

"Yeah, there's no need to move him, but I know I'll have to stay here and stabilise him first. You have enough to do."

"How important is this?"

"Very. For two reasons. The first is in how to treat his injuries—we need to know more about him."

"Wow."

"Yes, and the second reason you'll like. I think he can

tell us a great deal, not only about what happened in May 2013, but about Bill and Ben and other mysteries that I know you're keen to solve."

Meg felt a bolt of excitement. "How do you know he can help with these things?"

"Well, he was in the helicopter for a start, but also—he's different to us, Meg. He's human but different. I can't tell you more until I run the tests."

"What is his physical state now?"

"I'm only guessing, but I think he's—how can I explain? You've heard how doctors induce comas in some patients when they're seriously injured?"

Meg nodded.

"I think he's like that, but it's voluntary. It's like he's put himself in a state of suspension to help heal his body."

"That's amazing!"

"Yeah. I don't know how long this will last."

"You should go today."

"What?"

"If it's that important, you should go to the university today. We'll cope here."

"Are you sure?"

"Yup. I'd appreciate it if you look in on Connie first—I want your opinion."

"Oh, of course."

"How long will it take?"

"The tests? I'll have to get the generators going first, then run the preliminary work. The rest can be done on laptops back here. Three days, max. Yes, I'm sure I'll be back by nightfall in three days."

"Okay. Let's plan for that." She looked at the figure lying on the bed. His face, wrinkled and pale, was peaceful. It looked for all the world like he was sleeping.

CHAPTER FIFTEEN

As India poured fuel from a jerry-can into the small sedan, Meg ran inside to tell the others what was happening. Luke listened from the door to the bedroom, where his young wife still lay inert.

Her news was greeted with stunned silence, but the realisation that they all would now have to work twice as hard to cope with the temporary loss of Connie and India was received without complaint.

"Luke needs to sit with Connie, so I'll look after the animals. Heather, you're still chief baby-sitter, but I'm afraid you'll have less help. George—don't worry about any project work, just concentrate on the veggie patch, orchard and cooking." There were nods all around. "Hopefully India will be back quickly, and Connie will recover soon."

"So this guy in the shed, what does he look like?" Luke seemed excited.

"Old. Very old. His head is shaped a bit differently to ours."

"Wow. And what does India think he is?"

"She doesn't know. That's why it's so important she investigates quickly."

Heather was gazing out towards the shed. "Should we bring him here, into the house? It might make it easier to look after him."

"I don't know. I don't think that moving him at all is a good idea. Also, I'd rather know what we're dealing with before he lives right amongst us."

Heather nodded. They heard India's car skid in the dirt as it took off down the driveway.

"So, I'll keep an eye on both him and Connie, and take care of the animals. It's going to be a busy few days."

George had created two meals, one for the children, which he and Heather served to them in the early evening. The adults' meal was later, after the children were put to bed.

Delicious smells had been wafting through the house for a few hours, and everybody's stomachs were rumbling. Luke and Meg sat at the table while a smiling Heather helped George place the steaming bowls on the table. It was a risotto which George had served with some fish that had been caught in the dam and stored in the freezer. It was remarkable.

Luke scoffed his down with appreciation, and took a bowl in to Connie to see if she would rouse to eat any. He came back shaking his head, and then ate her portion.

Meg ate hers quickly and wondered if she should take any into the shed. The smell of the food might rouse the inert man. She dismissed this idea and helped herself to another plateful.

"Poor India. Imagine missing this meal. You outdid yourself, George. Congratulations."

George beamed. Luke heard the new baby girl stirring and went to look at her. Heather began clearing the table, and Meg leapt to her feet to help. They were surprised to see George running water into the sink for washing dishes. Meg winked at Heather and went back out to the shed.

The man hadn't moved, so Meg lifted a chair and carried it over to the bed quietly. She settled down with a book she found on India's work bench,—"Fundamentals of Dentistry." After turning a few pages she fell into a light sleep.

Something made her wake with a start. She looked around, disoriented for a moment, and then saw that the man's eyes were open. The first thing she noticed was their colour, which was startling. They were blue and green and a sort of light purple, all at once. Violet, blue and green. Then the man spoke.

"Ah, it's the lovely Meg. So nice to see your pretty face, my dear. Excuse me while I recover some more." The man closed his eyes again and returned to a state of suspension.

Meg sat open-mouthed for a moment. He knew her, knew her name? Her heart thudded violently in her chest. The man's voice had been cultured—urbane even. Like Cary Grant.

She wanted to shake him awake, ask him hundreds of questions. Restraining herself, she spread a blanket and pillow on the floor and opened her journal. It was a sad, but mysterious entry. A helicopter crash with two deaths and one survivor. A confinement with one death, one live child and the mother seriously ill. A stranger with something that piqued India's scientific curiosity so much that she'd driven one and a half hours to investigate. How strange it all was.

"Connie. Connie, honey. Can you wake up?"

Meg was shaking the young woman gently, but with no response. This was very worrying. It had been twenty-four hours since the birth, and Connie was still unconscious. A knot was forming in Meg's stomach. She didn't know what to do.

"Will she be all right?" Luke was pale, and his voice

was fretful.

"I just don't know, Luke. I must say I'm worried. Let's give her a few more hours and re-assess the situation."

Meg left Luke sitting by Connie's bedside and moved outside to milk the cows. After that, she checked the man in the shed and found his condition unchanged. She fed the animals and did some more chores. By then it was lunchtime.

The smell of freshly-baked bread greeted Meg as she entered the kitchen. George had laid out a spread of light refreshments and hot coffee. Meg ate hungrily and then kissed George on the cheek in appreciation. She took food in to Luke and then went back out to the shed.

As she sat next to the stranger again, he opened his remarkable eyes. He and Meg looked at each other for several seconds as the woman waited for him to talk.

"May I introduce myself? Excuse me if I don't stand—I'm not quite ready for that. I am...William."

Meg noted the hesitation the man had before stating his name, as though he had just thought of it.

"And I think you know me already. I'm Meg." She offered her hand, and he shook it without pressure.

"Yes. Of course you are. The lovely Meg. We are all so indebted to you."

Meg frowned. "Who are?"

"All of us. The descendants of Luke and Connie. You have helped us so much."

"I don't understand."

"No, sorry. I'm still a bit mind-addled. Of course you don't. I shouldn't be here, talking to you."

"Why not?"

"It's not done. I came to help Connie, but you weren't meant to see me. It's better that way."

"I don't understand. Why shouldn't I talk to you?"

"Because, I'm...well... I'm visiting you from a time in the future."

Meg stared at him, blinking. So that's what India was so excited about.

"But I guess it's too late now. You've seen me and you know where I'm from. I suppose I'll have to explain fully."

"Yes, please."

"Helping you now helps me and the others in my time. Poor Luke and Connie struggled on their own at first. We, their descendants, were suffering as a result."

"But I was there, helping all along."

"No, dear girl, you weren't."

"I don't understand."

William wriggled in the bed, trying to get comfortable. "I prefer the beds we have in the future." Meg waited for him to settle. "You see, we came back and put you here."

"Huh? What do you mean?"

"You were meant to die with the rest. The only survivors were the two young ones."

"So—how…"

"We went back and inoculated you against the virus that killed everyone else. When they died, you survived."

"And George, Heather, India, and John?"

"Yes, poor John. Sad loss. We found that just you and the young ones wasn't quite the right formula either, so we went back again—when we could—and inoculated them as well."

"When you could?"

"It's not often we can travel back, and each of us can only do it a limited number of times, you see. This might be my last time, so I've been here for a while, trying to help."

"Why didn't you just come and live with us?"

"That's never a good idea and I wasn't sure how you'd receive me. Instead I cloned the two men who piloted the helicopter. Unfortunately the results weren't wonderful and they were very clumsy."

"So there's no-one else in the whole rest of the world?"

A look came over the man's face that Meg couldn't decipher. "There are three others. No, one died. Just two now."

"Where are they?"

"The last I knew of them they were some distance from here. I doubt they'll ever find you. It was another of my little experiments that went wrong."

"Why?"

"They were brothers, you see. I was in a rush to select someone before I had to go back to my time and just gave the three of them injections."

"So, what's wrong with that?"

"I should have made sure of their personalities first. With you and the four others, I'd gone through a rigorous selection process. I found a database of psychometric tests—"

"Oh, like the one I did during a job interview?"

"Exactly. The four others had done these as well. That's how we chose you. But, not only that. We needed a geneticist, an expert on the environment, a builder and a school-teacher."

"Ah, I see."

"Your own psychometric test results were quite remarkable. Just what we needed. You can take on tasks, work out how to do them and then totally complete the task in a short time. Quite special."

"My old boss said I had a unique set of skills."

"Anyway, in the case of the three brothers, I had simply run out of time. I thought you could use more men, so I found the three of them..."

"So what's wrong with them?"

"They're—well, at best they're lacking in intelligence."

"And at worst?"

"I'd say they are slightly dangerous. I've been struggling with exactly what to do with them. One has already died, through misadventure."

"That sounds like a positive."

"I don't think the other two will last much longer. Gross stupidity in an unregulated world is a recipe for disaster."

"Gosh."

"Enough of that. The burning question for me is, how is Connie?"

Meg's shoulders slumped. "Not good. I'm at a loss."

"What are her symptoms?"

Meg described the birth and aftermath. William listened silently, nodding occasionally. Finally she finished.

"All right. We need to act quickly."

"You can help?"

"I hope so, but you'll need to support me."

"Sure. Name it."

"First of all, go to the helicopter wreckage and see what equipment is left. You're looking for a metal chest. You'll know it when you see it."

"Will I be able to carry it?"

"Yes, I think so. Also look for another container. It will be constructed of a material that looks like polyurethane to you."

"Okay."

"Go now, dear Meg. It should only take you a few minutes. I'll be waiting."

Meg nodded and waved goodbye. She ran to the house and told them she'd be back in a few minutes. Once in the vehicle, she realised she didn't know exactly where the wreck was.

She drove past her own house and then came to a spot where she thought the aircraft may have finally finished up. She was right.

After skidding to a stop, she climbed a fence and ran over to the wreckage. The bodies of Bill and Ben were still there, but it looked as though wildlife had been at their remains. She averted her eyes.

There was the metal box, still intact. The other one was open, however, and its contents were spread over a large area. She gathered up as many of the glass phials as she could and replaced them in the box. She made two trips to the car and then returned with a tarpaulin that she used to cover Bill and Ben.

As she sped past her own house, she wished she could shower and change clothing. That would have to wait. She drove back to the community house and sped up the driveway. George was in the vegetable patch.

"Hey, George. Can you help with these boxes?"

The big man hurried over and lifted the metal container and carried it easily over to the shed. Meg followed with the lighter, plastic one.

"Take it through to the bed, would you please?"

George hesitated.

"It'll be okay. William won't bite."

"William? Is that his name?"

"Yup. Come in quickly. I'll introduce you."

As their eyes adjusted to the dimmer light, they made out the figure of the old man on the bed.

"Oh it's George. I'm William. Pleased to meet you."

George moved forward and placed the box on the floor. He took William's hand, but seemed speechless.

"You and I will get to know each other later, George. For now I have to hurry and help Connie. Perhaps you can carry me to her?"

George nodded.

Meg looked around. "We could carry you in on a blanket, like a stretcher and put you on the bed next to Connie. I could run inside and get Luke to make room."

"Good girl. If George opens the metal box, I can check the equipment."

Meg ran inside and helped move Connie to the edge of the bed. By the time she returned to the shed, William had selected the medical gear needed. George counted to three and they hoisted the bedclothes up and carried the man into the house.

"Oh, the poor girl. She's so brave, our Connie." William looked close to tears. Luke stared at him with rapt attention. "And here's the wonderful Luke. Just put me down here, thank you both."

William went to work immediately. His tools were compact, with lights that shone various colours. One appeared to be a type of scanner, while the others seemed to be used as treatments. The minutes ticked by.

George excused himself and went back to the vegetable patch. Luke stood against a wall, not taking his eyes from his wife's face. Meg sat in a chair, trying to work out what William was doing.

Finally the old man sighed and lay back against a

pillow. He fell into a sound sleep.

Luke and Meg looked at each other. Meg raised her eyebrows and shrugged. She stood.

"Let me know if either one of them wakes, hey?"

Luke nodded and sat in the now-vacant chair. Meg patted him on the shoulder and returned to her jobs.

"Meg," said a small voice.

The woman looked down at Thomas, who was watching her do the afternoon milking. He was wearing rubber boots and a thick parka.

"Hi Tom. What's up?"

"Who's the man?"

Meg bit her lip. What was the best story for a child his age?

"He's someone who has come to help your mother."

"Is he a nice man? He looks old."

"Yes, he seems very nice and very old."

"He's sleeping in my Mum's bed."

"When he helped your mother, he tired himself out. He's been in an accident."

"How? What sort of accident?"

"Helicopter crash."

"With Bill and Ben?"

"Yes."

"Where are Bill and Ben?"

"Um, we think they died in the crash."

"Oh." Thomas was silent while he digested that information. "Ben gave me two jelly beans."

"Yes. You were very lucky."

Thomas looked at her for a moment, then his bottom lip began wobbling.

"What's wrong Thomas?"

"Ben died?"

"Yes."

"I'll never see him again?"

"No, I'm afraid not." She moved the milking stool to the next cow and began squeezing her teats. The milk gushed out in a hot flow.

A wailing sound make her look around. Thomas was running back to the house. He was crying loudly and saying, "Ben's dead. Ben's dead." Meg sighed. Perhaps she could have handled that one better.

Meg felt that she couldn't return to her own home that night, so after another delightful dinner and some murmured conversation with Heather and George, she settled herself in her old, original bed—the one she'd taken from a resort when she first arrived in Maleny—and fell into a deep sleep.

She was shaken awake by Luke. "Come quickly," he whispered. She was still fully dressed, so was on his heels when he walked into his and Connie's bedroom. William was still asleep, but Connie was sitting up, feeding the new baby girl.

"Well, that's a sight for sore eyes, I must say!" Meg spoke softly, not wanting to disturb the old man.

"Luke said he had been really worried, but I feel fine."

"I think William there worked some magic."

"Who exactly is he? Luke said you'd explain."

"Um, we don't know for sure yet. I'll find out and let you know later."

This didn't seem to worry the younger woman, who gazed down at her new daughter with an expression full of wonder.

"I'm sorry, Connie. We couldn't save the other baby." Meg felt tears welling in her eyes.

Connie smiled gently. "Don't blame yourself, for heaven's sakes. It's just the way it is. We're blessed with this little one, who we're naming Margaret, by the way."

"Oh, truly?" Meg's face beamed.

"Yes, because she seems so special, just like you."

Tears were running down Meg's cheeks. She looked at

the pair of them, so young, so proud in their parenthood. They'd had five children since finding each other after the virus killed everyone else. They were the special ones. The original survivors. She wanted to tell them about that, but thought she might save it until a later date.

Besides, she was still trying to come to terms with the information that William had given her. She should have died with the others. She wasn't sure yet how she felt about being saved. Grateful, she supposed.

There was so much more to learn from William, who was still sleeping soundly.

CHAPTER SIXTEEN

"Oh, no. Oh no." William was rummaging in the plastic box. He'd pick up one glass phial and fling it aside, before doing the same to the next.

"What's wrong?"

"It's all spoiled. All of it."

"What is it?"

"Food. My food. The container was damaged in the crash."

"But..."

"It's important. Oh, no. Look at it all!"

"Can't you eat our food?"

"Oh, gosh no. Don't even think it!"

"Why not?"

"I don't think I even could for a start."

"So, where can we get more of this special food?"

"Back where I was staying. The hospital in the desert."

"Where Luke and Connie and I were taken?"

"Yes."

"I don't know where that is."

"It's quite urgent, you know. Let me think. If you drove me to Maroochy airport, I could fly the jet out to the hospital."

"You can fly the jet?"

"Yes, well—I think so."

"You'd need someone to go with you."

"That may be wise. It would need to be you."

Meg sighed. She adjusted the roster in her head again. Connie was feeling better, so Luke could look after the animals.

"How long would we be gone?"

"If we leave now, we'd be back by nightfall."

"Just one thing. I must have a shower and change my clothes. It will take me half an hour."

William looked doubtful, but nodded. Meg ran out the door and drove home. She allowed herself a quick shampoo and stood under the warm water for a few extra moments. She shut the water off with regret, dried, and climbed into fresh clothes.

She pulled back into the driveway of the community house and drove straight up to the shed. William was waiting. She helped him climb into the four-wheel-drive and then ran to the house to tell them a heavily truncated version of what was happening.

An hour after that they were in the air, winging their way to a place west of Hughenden.

William groaned. "Oh, gosh. I forgot. We need to get from the airport to the hospital."

Meg searched her memory. "Last time there was a bus."

"Hmm, but I'm not sure it's actually at the airport."

"We'll know soon enough."

William nodded and adjusted the altitude of the jet. The sun was behind them, so it was pleasant flying. Meg was delighted in her bird's-eye view from the cockpit.

"It's such a beautiful flying day. It seems like we can see forever."

"Yes, dear girl. I've always enjoyed flight."

"Tell me about Connie—what you did for her."

William cleared his throat. "Well, it's complicated. I could tell you but there's no basis in your own medical knowledge for understanding. It would be gobbledygook."

Meg frowned. "But you fixed her. What was wrong?"

"So much. She was a mess. Minor bleed in the brain. Kidney damage—"

"Oh, gosh."

"Don't worry, she's fine now."

"You were able to fix her just like that?"

"Yes. I found some other minor things that weren't related to the birth and fixed those as well."

"You're a handy guy to have around."

William laughed. "For certain."

Meg wondered which of the hundred questions she should ask next. She didn't want to rush him.

"Is it just you who travels back to this time?"

"A colleague of mine has been back here as well. We'll call him, um, Martin. Last time I was back home, he was training another younger lad to come back. I think he— Martin that is—has only one more turn left."

"I notice you hesitate when using your names. Why is that?"

"Oh, because we are known by other names in the future. A series of numbers and letters that you would find confusing. Martin and I gave each other 2013 names."

"How many of you are there—in the future? Oh, and what is the date there?"

"Time is such a flexible thing, my dear. It's a hard question to answer. Let's say for the sake of argument that I exist four to five hundred or so years hence. There was originally fewer than one thousand of us, although the population has grown since we put you with Luke and Connie, and then again when we added the other four."

Meg frowned. "How do you mean?"

"It's complicated and hard to imagine, but I'll try. When Luke and Connie were the only survivors, they had an awful time just even getting to each other. They both nearly died, and it was only their extreme youth that saved them. It took them a long time to recover and then to procreate. Their offspring weren't healthy. This actually damaged their DNA—India can tell you about that."

"So the further generations were unhealthy?"

"Yes. Adding you to the picture made us feel better immediately. Suddenly there were more of us. That's when we decided to add four more."

"And what happened then?"

"Oh, it was exciting! India made a big difference in her lifetime. The effect of adding her was incredible. We were healthier and more energetic. We were so much stronger. I can't tell you what a difference it made."

"So then you added three more men."

"Yes." He sighed. "Ah, well. We all make mistakes."

Meg wondered what the next question should be, but was interrupted.

"Here, we go. That's Hughenden down there. I'll just

circle around and check out the airport."

The jet banked and circled. "Ha! We're in luck—the bus is there."

He levelled out and then began a descent. Soon they were taxiing to the bus. The jet had built-in steps that deployed when the door was opened.

"Let's go. I'm starving!" William was rubbing his hands together.

"Give it a rest and try turning the engine over again in a few minutes."

Meg looked at William wearily. It was hot and dusty and she'd been trying to start the bus for the past half hour. She could see the desperation in the man's face. He needed his special food.

"I'm going to have to walk there, aren't I?" Her voice was low. She was hoping he'd have another solution.

"We could try taxiing the jet along the dirt road for a while, but it's a risk. If a tyre became damaged..."

"Yes. I understand. I'll start off straight away. I should just be able to follow the dirt road right to the hospital, right?"

"That's right, but if the road isn't clear, stay headed toward that rise. That's Mt Walker that sits beyond the hospital, but it's a straight line from here to the hospital and then the mountain."

"Okay."

"What a wonderful girl you are."

"Flattery's good, I suppose."

William chuckled. He gave her a description of what she needed to bring back, and it didn't seem too bad, the way he explained it.

Meg waved and began walking. Soon she was terribly hot and thirsty. The thought of having water at the hospital kept her putting one foot in front of the other. The heat was dry—a change from the humidity in Maleny—so she didn't find it quite as energy-sapping.

After more than an hour, the building came into view. She jogged the last hundred metres or so and burst inside for shade and water. She ran one tap, but the water was brown. Another produced better results and she drank thirstily, hoping she wasn't poisoning herself.

The supplies William needed were where he suggested they would be. He explained that the items couldn't be transferred to another container—the boxes were sealed to keep the contents fresh. He asked her to collect one box of each of the four colours. She lifted them onto a bench first, one by one in a stack. Then she lifted all four. She could *just* carry them. Figuring she'd have to make another trip if she didn't take all four at once made her keen to succeed.

It took a lot longer on the return journey, not helped by the fact she couldn't see over the stack of containers. She almost tripped on plants several times. Once she half-fell into a pothole, but kept the stack steady. The jet was a welcome sight.

"Ah, wonderful Meg. I was beginning to get concerned for you." He helped her to unload, then clasped her hand. "Thank you, dear girl."

Meg watched him open one of the containers and noted the care he took to do it in a particular way. She guessed it was in order to preserve the remaining contents after he'd consumed what he needed to.

He had removed three flasks and uncorked and drank all of them in a very short time. Some colour began returning to his face. "Ah, that's better. You're a lifesaver, Meg."

"Well, I guess I owed you one after saving me from the virus."

"I hadn't thought about it in that way. Okay, we're even now." He stood with restored energy and climbed down the aircraft steps. He looked toward the west.

"Ah, what a shame. It's too late to fly back to Maroochy in daylight."

"You can't fly at night?"

"If I was confident of this aircraft, I'd attempt it. I'm thinking it might be prudent to wait until morning. These seats should be comfortable." He fiddled with some controls. The back of the seat moved into a flat position. "Ah. We'll be very comfortable, I think."

"I don't suppose there's any water on board here."

"Good question. Here's a refrigerator."

There was juice, soft drink, and wine. Meg checked the use by dates and decided that the soft drink was the best option out of the non-alcoholic drinks. She opened one and began chugging it down. After a few minutes, a huge burp erupted. Meg laughed and excused herself.

Above the refrigerator were crisps and nuts. She didn't check the dates, but began eating hungrily. William watched her with amusement.

Meg adjusted another of the passenger seats until it lay almost flat. She was lying, facing William who was across the narrow aisle. She began thinking about more questions, but instead slipped into oblivion.

CHAPTER SEVENTEEN

"Hey, we're home. Where is everybody?"

She walked through to the back of the house and then looked outside. Connie was walking slowly in the soft, afternoon sunshine, carrying the baby. She looked to be singing to it softly. Luke was feeding a baby lamb with a bottle, while Maisie stood with a hand on his knee, watching in wonder. George was in the vegetable patch, checking the undersides of the lettuces. Heather had the children sitting in a circle and appeared to be telling them a story.

William came and stood at Meg's side. "A pretty picture, no?"

"Yes, indeed. Quite lovely." They stood in silence for a few more minutes. "I should get your food from the car."

"No rush, my dear. It will be all right in there. One of the men can lift it out in a while."

Meg looked around for India's car. It was nowhere to be seen. She counted the days on her fingers and thought that the other woman should arrive back by nightfall—at the latest. Meg couldn't wait to tell her all that she'd learned from William.

She moved into the kitchen and drank deeply from a jug of water. Then she found some bread and broke a hunk off.

When she walked back to the living room, William was still standing in the same position. He was smiling. Meg noticed the straighter carriage and could almost feel the change in his energy.

"I'll take you out and introduce you to everyone."

"Hush, girl. Just stand still and watch." Meg re-joined him at the window. "You don't know how lucky you are, the beauty of the world you're living in. This is just perfect."

"Yes, I suppose it is."

"Don't take it for granted. Don't take anything for granted. You are one of the blessed ones. We in the future are quite jealous you know."

"Why?"

"Because you still know how to enjoy yourselves. Don't think I didn't smell that wonderful food that was being prepared the other night. Ours is—well, you've seen it. We have one of those phials once or twice per day. I had three yesterday to make up for what I'd missed. It is a miracle product. Contains everything our bodies need. It even has a pleasant taste—you actually have a choice of four distinct flavours."

"Oh, I see. The different coloured trim on the boxes."

"Yes, but I've seen the old movies—banquets being prepared and eaten with pleasure. Wines being matched with food. Entrees and main courses and desserts and cheese plates."

"What would happen to you if you tried to eat them?"

"I think the results would be catastrophic. We humans of the future decided that the procurement, preparation and eating of food was too time consuming, and too hit-and-miss in terms of nutritional benefits. We needed quantifiable results. At the same time, we automated much of what had to be done in our world. We actually have next-to-nothing to do and all day to do it."

"Hard to imagine."

"None of us are overweight, because that food we have balances the kilojoules and energy required. It is even tailored especially for each individual, depending on energy used."

"Wow. That's impressive."

"No. I'll tell you what's impressive. George there, growing beautiful vegetables. Making soups and juices and sauces. Luke raising animals and birds that can be eaten for the protein needed. I can help you with cheese-making, by the way."

"Oh, how did you come across that skill?"

"I looked it up before I came back this time. A quicker and easier method was found around a hundred years from now."

"Excellent!" Meg looked at him and smiled, and was rewarded with a warm smile in return. He was looking younger and healthier all the time. "It's time to meet them now—no more excuses."

"Lead on, darling Meg."

It was only Heather and the children who still had to meet William. Heather greeted him a bit uncertainly, but the children took to him immediately.

George was astonished by the change in the older man. "It looks like you've swallowed some magic pills there William. I wouldn't mind a few myself."

William laughed. "I was just saying to Meg how lucky you people are to have all this wonderful fresh food and a great chef like yourself to prepare it."

Meg could see George's chest expand. "You can join our dinner table now you're up and about."

"Sadly no. Meg will explain. For the moment I'd just love to walk around this beautiful property and pat some animals."

Thomas and Maisie walked up to him. "Can we come too?"

"Of course. Oh, if it's all right with your parents?" Luke and Connie smiled and nodded, and the three of them set off into the orchard.

"Well, he looks nice enough." Heather sounded like she was trying to convince herself.

George didn't hesitate. "A wonderful man. I hope he stays around for a while. So where did you say he's from?"

"Well..."

"Those eyes of his, and his head shape. He's not really like one of us."

"He is and isn't. I don't know the full details, but will let you know as soon as I do."

"Fair enough."

Heather poked George with her elbow. "I'd like to know more about him before he has a lot to do with the children."

"Good point." George looked enquiringly at Meg.

"He's come to help us. If I had children here, I wouldn't hesitate to let them be around him as much as they wanted."

There was a spare place at the dinner table. India hadn't arrived back. William sat in her place for a while, but then begged tiredness and went into the shed.

"I wonder where India has got to. She seemed fairly certain of how long the process would take."

Heather covered Meg's hand with her own. "Don't worry. India is a very capable person."

"I know that, but it's not like her to be back later than she says."

"That's true. She'd know you would worry about her."

Meg's concern prevented the full enjoyment of George's lamb shanks that were slow cooked in red wine. Connie, however, enjoyed hers so much that she ate seconds and then requested thirds. They were served with fluffy mashed potatoes that soaked up the juices in the most spectacular way.

"The meat just falls off the bone, George." Connie sighed and had another mouthful. "It's just heaven."

"Here, here." Luke was on his second serving.

Meg pushed her chair back from the table and walked out to the shed. The light was on and William was lying on the bed, staring at the dentistry book. He lowered it when Meg walked in.

"I'm worried about India, William."

"She was due back some time ago, wasn't she?"

"Yes, and it's uncharacteristic."

"Do you know which way she would have driven?"

"Um, yes. Mostly."

"Then it's an easy decision. If she's not back by lunchtime tomorrow, go searching."

Meg blew out her cheeks. "Gosh, yesterday and today it was flying out to the desert in a jet. Tomorrow a drive to Brisbane. I'll wear out!"

"I'll come with you."

"Do you think you're up to it?"

"Certainly. How long a drive is it?"

"Oh, I guess one and a half hours each way."

"The jet wouldn't help then. Too short a distance."

"True."

"Don't worry, dear girl. Something will happen. It always does."

Meg laughed. "Yes, but what?"

Meg returned to her own house that night. She was bone-weary, but washed herself thoroughly before going to bed—cleaning the desert dust from her skin. She applied several coats of cooling moisturiser to some sunburn, and then groaned in pleasure at the sensation of climbing under the sheets of her own bed.

Her journal beckoned. She had missed one entry, so recounted the events of two days. Her eyelids began closing.

Sleep didn't come quickly however. Her overtired brain kept wanting to work on the problem of India. Where was she? Was she in trouble? Maybe she didn't even arrive at UQ. She wished they had a system of communication under these circumstances. What would work? She was tempted to drive back to William at the other house and ask his opinion.

After a fitful night of sleep she ended up waking late. The sun was already high in the sky. She cursed and got ready quickly, driving to the community house without delay. She frowned when she couldn't see India's car.

Connie was in the kitchen, kneading bread dough. George was watching her carefully. "Oh hi, Meg. George is sharing his baking secrets with me. I'm going to start preparing breakfast and lunches again, as well as the kiddies' dinner. George will keep cooking ours, by popular demand."

"That's all good. No one has seen India?"

"No. She'll be back soon. You know how she gets when she's in the middle of a project. She's so focused that she often forgets to eat, even."

"Maybe, Connie. But I'm still worried. If she's not back soon, I'll grab an early lunch and head off to find her."

"Oh, okay. Yes, that might be best."

"William will come as well."

"Good. You never know what might happen."

"Are you ready for a road-trip?" Meg asked William.

"Certainly."

"We should only be gone for the day, but we've already seen how things can go wrong. Pack food for two or three days."

"Yes, wise advice."

"I'll go and prepare some food for myself and India. Are you coming over to the house?"

"No, I'll wait here. Come and get me when you're ready."

CHAPTER EIGHTEEN

Meg cursed when heavy rain began falling just south of Beerwah. It would have been such a quick and easy drive in normal conditions. She adjusted her speed and settled further into her seat.

William pulled his seatbelt into position and clicked the buckle into place. "Don't trust my driving, eh?" Meg's smile was mischievous.

"It's not that," said William, but didn't offer another reason.

He clearly enjoyed the drive, commenting on landmarks along the way. At Nambour she took him past the Big Pineapple, a replica of the spiky fruit, made from fibreglass. At Palmview she pointed out the Ettamogah Pub and told William about its background as a setting for a cartoon.

The kilometres sped by, and the rain became heavier. Finally they were on the western side of Brisbane, and Meg was following the signs to the University of Queensland.

The campus looked impressive even in bad weather, but it was only William who noticed. Meg was too busy trying to find the building that India would be working in.

Finally it was before them in all its sandstone glory. India's car was nowhere in sight. "Stay here, I'll run inside."

"I have an easier way." William already had a device sitting on his knees. It was like a laptop, but without a full keyboard, just some buttons. He pressed one of these and the screen began displaying the outline of a building that Meg realised was the one before them. William pressed another button and there was movement on the screen, like scanning. This movement only lasted a matter of seconds. "There's no-one in that building."

"She also mentioned a genome research place, separate to her laboratory. I don't know if it's in this campus or not." Fortunately they found a sign which pointed to the facility, not far from where they were. India wasn't there either.

Meg drove around the streets of the campus for another fifteen minutes, trying to catch sight of the car. Finally, she sighed and sped out to the main road. "Let's see if we can find her on the way home."

After a few minutes she pulled over and looked at the map again. "I have to think like India. Which way would she go?"

"The most direct route. She's a practical and unemotional woman."

Meg lifted her brows at William. He smiled. "You forget, I saw her psychometric profile."

"Of course, and you're quite right. She would make a beeline for home and wouldn't be distracted by things to see."

The kilometres sped by quickly. The skies were now spewing water with a vengeance. The wipers were on full speed and Meg leaned closer to the windscreen to improve the vision.

As they came past the massive Chermside Shopping Centre, William suggested they slow down. "We need to watch for clues."

"Why here. Why not back there?"

"You might call it a hunch."

As they came to Aspley, there was a sign painted on a sheet, and this was hung over a large road sign which indicated a turn-off to Albany Creek. The rain-soaked paint was streaking, but still legible. "HELP MEDICLE ASISTNACE NEEDED!"

"Here we go." William's voice had a tone of satisfaction, as though he'd been expecting just this outcome.

Two further signs led Meg and William to a mansion on

acreage. India's car was clearly visible.

"Stop here. Back up a few metres." William's voice sounded urgent.

Meg hadn't had time to think this through, but as they sat and watched the house, the penny dropped. "The brothers!"

"Yes, indeed."

"Lacking intelligence, could be dangerous."

"To themselves and others."

"What will we do?"

"Nothing just yet." He pulled out the laptop-type device. They both watched as the scanning was performed. Three figures glowed. William grunted. "Are you feeling brave, Meg?"

Meg looked at him levelly. "Let me guess. I'm to go and knock on the front door as diversion."

"You're definitely smarter than the average."

"What are you going to do?"

"I'm guessing that India is the figure by herself in another room. I'd like to check this out while the men are talking to you."

"Sure. We should have brought weapons."

"Of course, my dear." He patted his pocket.

"What is it?"

His eyes twinkled. "You'll see."

Meg took a deep breath and opened the car door. The rain had lessened to a gentler shower. She whistled as she walked to feign a relaxed attitude. Nobody looked out windows at her that she could see.

She knocked loudly. After a minute the door swung open.

The man was very thin, but in strange contradiction, had a large belly. He was dressed in a checked flannelette shirt and blue jeans. A cap was turned backward on his head. His hair and beard were long and greasy.

"Well, well, well. What do we 'ave 'ere?"

"I saw a sign saying you needed medical help."

"Yeah, but he died."

"Oh, I'm sorry. So you don't need me then?"

The man smiled, showing rotting teeth. "Come inside. We could still use your 'elp."

The interior of the house was a horrendous mess. Bottles and cans were strewn all over the floor. There were empty chip packets and other junk foods adding to the chaos. Meg thought she saw a rodent run through a pile of rubbish in the entry.

"Do you live here alone?" She kept her voice light and innocent.

"Nah, me brovver is 'ere as well."

Another figure emerged from the dark interior. He was dressed the same as the first and also had the long hair and beard. "Hey, that means we 'ave one each now. Cool!"

Meg thought she heard a noise at the rear of the house, but the men seemed oblivious. They both moved until they were standing together, facing her. Their backs were to the window and Meg saw a figure darting toward her car. She was careful not to follow it with her eyes.

"What do you mean, one each? Is there someone else here?"

The brothers looked at each other and laughed. The one on the right clutched his right cheek. "Ow, that 'urts."

"I thought she was gonna fix it for ya!"

"A friggin' abscess, she reckons. Says she'll 'ave to pull the tooth."

"Faark. What about drugs?"

"Reckons she can get some stuff, and some pullin' tools. Said she'd drive off and get some."

"What did you say?"

"Said she had to scratch an itch I 'ad first." The brothers laughed. "Then I told 'er she'd 'ave to scratch yours too."

"What did she say?"

"Nuffin. I heard you talkin' so came out to see what was up." He grinned at Meg. "Now the ovver one just has to do me."

Meg listened to this conversation with something approaching amusement. Obviously nothing bad had happened to India yet, and Meg figured she was now sitting in Meg's car. But where was William?

"Reckon we should take this one in with the ovver one and 'ave a bit of a party. Take some beer as well—to lubricate things, right?"

"Dunno. Do ya like beer, girlie?"

"Champagne, thanks fellas." They laughed.

"Oh, hang on!" One of the brothers moved into another room. They heard him opening and closing doors. "Da-da!" he said, proudly holding a bottle of French champagne aloft.

"It has to be cold."

"Eh? Nup. No power 'ere."

"Do you like your beer warm?" He shook his head. "Well, don't like my champagne warm either. Besides, if you open that bottle at this temperature..."

The man peeled the foil from the top and undid the wire fastener. He leaned over the bottle and began levering the cork with his thumbs. It needed little encouragement, shooting out and hitting him hard in the eye.

"Ow, ow, ow. It's blinded me!"

His brother sighed. "Look, it's spilling out everywhere, you idiot."

"Don't call me an idiot!"

Holding his sore eye, he launched himself at his brother. They began rolling around the floor, squashing cans and breaking bottles in the process. One of the men, Meg didn't know which, rolled onto a shard of glass which cut deeply into his back, around where the kidneys lay. He screamed.

Meg realised William was by her side. He shook his head and raised a small tube. A beam of light struck one brother and he became still. The other brother looked on in puzzlement. William aimed the tube again. Two men lay in the mess together.

"Where did you get to?"

"I just wanted to listen for a moment. Two lives are fairly precious here and now. I hoped there was a chance I could salvage the situation. Give them some meaningful work." He shook his head. "They were beyond help." He looked down at the device and pressed another button. This time a red ray hit the men and reduced each to a pile of ash. "It's a sad day."

"India's okay?"

"Yes, very calm. We'd better go now." William clicked his tongue in disgust as he made his way to the front door. "Just like animals. No—worse."

Meg ran down to the road and opened India's door. "I'm so glad to see you!"

The other woman smiled calmly. "Me too. I'll follow you home in my car."

"You're okay to drive?"

"Of course!"

"So you met William..."

"Nice man. Great genes."

"Great jeans?"

"The other kind of genes, silly. I'll tell you when we get home."

CHAPTER NINETEEN

Meg's fountain pen was moving swiftly across the pages of her journal. So much to tell:

"And India has told me about his DNA, how advanced he is and in what ways. She didn't need to tell me about his increased intelligence, I'd already worked that one out. That man has intelligence to burn. I find that very attractive. He is certainly superior to any man I've known.

He is old, but seems fit (now that he has begun eating again). I've caught him doing some sort of workout that might have origins in eastern martial arts. He seems to be increasing his workout time daily.

I love the way he talks, too. Love his voice...."

She stopped writing and re-read the last three paragraphs. What was this—the gushing of a lovesick schoolgirl? She went to rip the pages from the book, but stopped herself. She crossed out the lines instead.

There was a knock on her bedroom door. "Come in, India. I'm awake."

"Your place is cool. I love it. Look at that view!"

India had stayed over at Meg's the night before so they could talk about the results of the genome sequencing and what it meant in terms of their community. Meg told her about how Luke and Connie were the original survivors, and how the rest of them were saved to support them. She and India also discussed the confusing thought that whatever they did now could so dramatically change what was going to happen to mankind in the future.

India had paused for a moment, considering her next words carefully. "It's what John always said, you see."

"What?"

"It doesn't matter whether there's only the tiny group of us, or seven billion as there was back in 2013. Whatever we do now affects the future population, don't you see?"

"Ah, I get it. But it seems so much more important now."

"Not necessarily. Think for a minute. Where did this virus come from?"

"William said something about the polar ice caps."

"So the virus was exposed because the ice-caps were melting, right?"

"Um, yeah."

"Think, Meg. Why were they melting?"

"Global warming."

"Caused by..."

"Pollution?"

"It's CO2. Carbon dioxide. Acts like a blanket and traps the heat in."

"Yeah, so?"

"So, if we had listened to the warnings—and there were plenty of those—and cut CO2 emissions—"

"The virus would have stayed trapped in the ice?"

"Precisely."

"So? Sorry, I forgot the point."

"You're saying that what our little group does now radically affects William and the people of the future. I'm saying that what mankind has been doing for years affected things more dramatically than that. It just about killed everybody off."

"All except Luke and Connie."

"Yes."

"How do you feel about being saved by William and his people, now that you've had time to think about it?"

India shrugged. "I'm here. It doesn't matter how it happened." Meg had smiled at this typical India response.

Now the scientist was standing at the edge of the mezzanine in Meg's bedroom, looking over the strange mountains to the coast. She turned and smiled. "It's a wonderful day to be alive. Let's go and chat some more to William."

William smiled in satisfaction. "You have an excellent mind, India. I can see you're soaking up all of this like a sponge."

India placed the cap carefully back on the felt-tipped pen she always used. "Well, it's like this. No one in this world, up to this time, has had the opportunity to hear anything like this. It's just incredible. You guys should have gone back further and influenced decision-makers a long time ago."

"Sadly we couldn't. We've been very limited in what we could do in terms of travelling backward. It's been hit-and-miss and highly dangerous. We can only do it occasionally, when all the right things align in the universe. We've been lucky to have achieved what we have."

India nodded. "Yes, I see." She uncapped her pen again and asked some questions based in science that Meg had no understanding of. She began to feel left out. No, it was more than that. India and William had a bond that Meg couldn't share. It was scientific knowledge. This realisation made Meg feel slightly ill. She excused herself and ran out of the shed. As she left, she heard the conversation continue as if she hadn't moved.

"Well, everyone. We've invited William along to this meeting because it's time to explain exactly who he is and what his presence here means to all of us." Meg scanned the room and found pleasure in the way everyone, especially Luke and George, leaned forward in their seats.

This meeting had been troublesome. Meg had been concerned about how much to tell the others, and asked India her opinion. The other woman had looked at her levelly. "The truth, Meg. Simple."

"But it's a bit overwhelming."

"It's the truth. Pure and simple. You can't get into trouble or cause problems if you don't try to hide anything."

"How about how they were meant to die but were saved by injections?"

"Sure."

"I reckon the concept of time travel doesn't even faze you. You probably did a paper on it or something."

India smiled in her maddening calm way. "No, no paper. But yes, as scientists, we discussed the probability that it would eventually happen."

"You said probability, not possibility."

"Yes, that's right."

"You see what I mean? It was already real in your mind

before William came to us. The rest of us had no idea."

"Oh, I'm not too sure about that. Luke is a sci-fi fan. George is just a big kid. They'll love it."

"How about Connie and Heather?"

"They'll just have to come to terms with it. Won't they?"

Now, as Meg looked around the room, she realised she was about to have some fun.

"William here, came to us in order to help Connie with her childbirth. Sadly, the helicopter crashed. William was injured but was able to recover." Luke looked at Meg with an attitude of impatience.

"What we now know is this: William is from—"

"I know!" said George, jumping from his seat. "I worked it out!"

Meg frowned. "Okay, George. Tell us."

"Another planet. He came to help us from, I dunno, Mars or something."

"Um, no. But it was a good guess." George sat heavily in his chair again. Heather patted him on the leg. "Anyone else want to throw some theories forward?" There was silence. "Okay. So William came to us from ... the future."

Four pairs of eyes turned bigger and swung toward William, who smiled and nodded.

"But that's not all. He told me, and India, what killed everyone and what happened next." There was a collective gasp.

"Tell us!" cried Luke.

"I'm going to give the floor to William for that explanation."

The time traveller, in his smooth, modulated voice, explained about the virus that had been trapped for so long in the ice-caps. It regenerated when the ice began melting and then mutated. It was in the general population for a short time before it had a flash of exposure. He then told of how there were only two humans left in the world.

"Two?" Connie looked puzzled.

Meg took the floor back. "It was you and Luke, Connie. You were the original survivors. But life was tough and you didn't flourish. The people in William's time developed a vaccine for the virus and came back to inoculate us to help you."

"Wow!" Connie smiled at William. "Thank you."

George scratched his head and looked at Heather. She shrugged. "I don't get it," he said.

"Yes, it took me a few minutes too, George. That's why I thought I'd explain it, and not India or William. You see, you were meant to die, but the time travellers came back and gave you a jab, like the fluvax. This was before May 2013. That way you survived and were able to come and help here."

"Incredible. Amazing." George looked flabbergasted. "But why me? Why any of us?"

William cleared his throat. "Do you remember completing a psychometric test, both of you?"

Heather nodded. George frowned. "Oh, there was something when I went for a job at a big construction company. Weird questions. Lots of them."

"Yes, that's it. We chose you based on those results."

George nodded and fell silent. Meg smiled at him. "This is all good news of course, because now we have William living among us. Guess what? He can show us an easy way to make cheese!"

Everybody smiled at that welcome news.

"Thanks for being so patient while we worked all of this out. Now we'll have some coffee and a lovely cake that George baked. Tiramisu, did you say?" George smiled and nodded. "You can all ask William or India any questions—they're better on the scientific stuff than me." Meg said this bravely, recognising the sinking feeling in her stomach as the truth was so clearly stated.

Luke and George ignored the refreshments and made a beeline for William. Heather seemed stunned and unable to move. Connie fetched the cake and coffee. Life went on.

CHAPTER TWENTY

"So tell me William, in what other ways do we indulge in more pleasure that you guys do in your time?"

Meg felt a bit tipsy. They'd had a magnificent Italian feast, which George had served with some astonishingly good red wine. Alcohol hadn't passed Meg's lips since she and India were caught without water after the car broke down. Even William had taken a sip to see what the fuss was about. Then he'd come back for another mouthful.

Now the two of them, William and Meg, were at her house. Meg had set up a table and chairs out on the wooden deck that jutted over the water of the dam. They were dressed against the cold, and shivering slightly.

"So many ways, darling Meg. We have this strange attitude that we have deserved our enforced leisure. Machines do all our work. Do you know how boring that is?"

Meg frowned. She couldn't remember the last time she was bored.

"In any case, pleasure can be gained from meaningful

employment. For me, experiments, reading and writing keep me amused."

"And your friend, Martin. What does he do?"

"Similar. That's how we became friends."

"How about physical pleasure?"

"Yes, I believe in the benefits of daily exercise. It's good for the brain as well as the body."

Meg frowned. Was he deliberately ignoring the question?

"No, I mean—you know—between men and women."

William looked at Meg for the longest time, it seemed. Several heartbeats at least. "Oh, you mean the act of sexual intercourse?"

"Well, yes. That and other things."

"What other things?"

Meg took a deep breath and ploughed on. "Other forms of sexual pleasure. And just nice things like kissing and cuddling."

"No. We don't do that."

"What, nothing?"

"That's considered, well...primitive. We procreate in other ways."

"How?"

"In vitro. We use the best scientific methods so that

the outcomes are less—"

"Hit-and-miss?"

"Exactly, Meg. I knew you'd understand."

"But I don't."

"Oh?"

"You've got no idea, have you—what you're missing out on?"

"How do you mean?"

She leaned forward and placed her lips against his. At first she met resistance, but then his mouth softened. They began several minutes of very passionate kissing.

She pulled away. "See?"

"Hmm. I see. Yes, I must admit that's rather nice."

Meg felt emboldened. She reached under the layers of clothing and undid her bra. She moved her chair until it was level with his but facing him. She took his hand and guided under her clothing. She felt his hand contract over the breast, feeling it. Then he narrowed his grasp until he had her nipple between his fingers. He squeezed the nipple gently, which made her groan. It had been so long.

"So you've never slid into the warm wetness of a woman?"

"No," he said with a smile. "But something tells me I'm just about to."

Meg woke smiling. She yawned and stretched. The release from sexual tension was an experience she hadn't had for some time, and she was now basking in it.

William had proven to be an enthusiastic student. Once he'd sampled the pleasure a woman's body could give him, he wanted more. And more. Meg couldn't remember a time she'd been so thoroughly pleasured.

She had insisted that he should go back to the community house and wanted to drive him. He, however, decided he wanted to walk. "I feel so young, my gorgeous woman. I could run for one hundred kilometres. I want to sample the night like I sampled your body. My heavens, what delights!" He had certainly been profuse in his gratitude. She'd warned him about being circumspect. It was nobody else's business but theirs, their lovemaking. "Whatever you say, you gorgeous woman."

She now ran her hands over her belly and breasts, wanting to experience how they'd felt to him. Beautiful and silky smooth. No wonder he'd been so excited.

She reached for her journal and wrote page after page until her hand cramped. She was the happiest she'd been in so many years. She couldn't remember the last time. Had she ever been so happy?

She was singing as she showered, humming as she dressed. She ate breakfast quickly and drove to the other house. Today she wanted to begin a new project.

"A schoolhouse you say?" George looked puzzled.

"Yeah, for Heather when she's teaching. There are just so many children now, and India hasn't had hers yet. Heather's trying to teach them in the lounge room and it's just not working."

"Ah, yes. I see. Have you drawn plans?"

"No, but I can sort of see it. How about you and I think about it today and we'll discuss plans tonight."

"Sure thing. It sounds good."

Meg saw India walking toward her, holding her belly. "Hi! Everything alright?"

"Yeah, I think so. Slight contractions. I had them last time."

"Like Braxton Hicks?"

"Yeah. I had them for at least a week before Peter and Marie were born."

"That's good. I was just talking to George about a schoolhouse. After your babies come into the world we'll have so many children they'll be impossible to teach in the house."

"Great idea. I'm sure it won't be long before Connie and Heather are pregnant again either."

"Gosh, I hope not. Poor Connie. I'm not sure she should do that again."

"Try telling her that."

"Perhaps I should talk to Luke."

"Maybe."

"If William was staying on I wouldn't be so concerned. You should have seen him fix Connie up."

"Yes, well I wouldn't count on him sticking around."

"Oh?" Meg feigned indifference, but her heart began beating so fast she was afraid that the other woman would hear it.

"Well, there's the issue of his food, for a start. He'll need more eventually."

"I reckon you could find a way to produce something that could take its place."

"Maybe. Maybe not. Then there is the talk of the short windows they have for travelling. I think if he misses his trip home, he'll be marooned here. I'm not sure he'd like that."

"Perhaps he'll come to like it."

"I'm not sure about that. Anyway, I don't think we should encourage Connie toward pregnancy again in the hope that William can come to her rescue."

"Sure. That's sensible. Have you seen William this morning?"

"He was asleep when I went into the shed, so I left him there. He's normally awake by now."

"Yes, we sat up talking for ages. Then he walked home."

"Good on him! Anyway, when he wakes up I want to run some formulae past him. I'm quite excited by them. I just don't believe what I'm learning." She winced and rubbed her belly. "Damned contractions."

"Oh, Meg. That would be so wonderful!" Heather's smile was radiant. "It's been very hard to teach in the lounge room, and it's only going to get worse as the kids grow older."

"I could see that. You should have suggested it yourself!"

"The thought occurred every now and again, but I was just too busy to form any sort of real idea."

"I can understand that. Here is a rough sketch I drafted. What do you think?"

"Has George seen it yet?"

"No, I wanted your input before he takes the project over."

Heather smiled. "Good idea." She took the drawing

book from Meg and considered the plans.

Meg looked around the house. It was messy but comfortable. The children were unusually quiet, some having naps, while others played contentedly. It was a rare moment.

Heather drew some lines on the plan and wrote some comments with arrows. "I love the open plan, Meg. Great for this climate. Those sliding panels will be good in winter. I'd just like a small room here for supplies. That's all."

"I'm glad you like it." The two women smiled at each other. Meg had a thought. "Are you using contraception now?"

"Yeah, absolutely. I couldn't do another pregnancy yet."

"Ever?"

"Um, I guess so. It's so funny—the way it's worked out."

"How?"

"The way things were going in my life—you know, before 2013, it didn't look like I was going to have any children."

"Why not?"

Heather picked some fluff from her dress. "The man I was seeing, I don't think he would have wanted children."

"What made you think that?"

"He was older than me, by fourteen years. He already had children—three—to his wife."

"Wife?"

"Soon to be ex-wife."

Meg blinked. "He was married?" Wow. India was right. This woman was more than she appeared.

"Yeah." Heather took a deep breath. "It didn't start like that It all began with professional interest." Her words began to tumble out quickly. "He was teaching at the same school. We had students in common and we found it useful to meet up in the teachers' room after school ended for the day and discuss them."

"Sounds innocent enough."

"Oh, it was always innocent. We didn't have an affair."

"So?"

"How can I explain it? One day a contractor came to build cupboards in the teachers' room and this interrupted our meeting. Philip suggested we go to a local coffee shop. Then we began meeting there two afternoons a week."

"And?"

"The school holidays came and I missed our meetings. Time went by. A couple of years—"

"You met in a coffee shop twice a week for two years?" Meg smiled.

"Sounds funny, I know. I waited for him to make a move—"

"What would you have done?"

Heather looked at the floor, frowning. "I was fairly fond of him. I'm not sure. Didn't really want anything messy. If we had an affair I'd be the loser in the long term. If he left his wife there would be maintenance payments and upset children."

"So, what happened?"

"One child had already left home when we first began meeting. Over those couple of years, the other two children also left home and became independent."

"So there wouldn't be maintenance payments and all those things."

"Yes. Another school year finished and I was faced with eight weeks without meeting him. I wasn't happy."

"That's sad."

"But one day there was a knock at my door—a Thursday morning. There he was. We drank coffee on my balcony and he told me a story about seeing one of the students in the supermarket—caught him shoplifting. Said he just had to tell me, and that he missed our meetings. He'd remembered where I said I lived—"

"So that's when you began an affair?"

"No. He began coming to my place twice a week. Around halfway through the holidays I had to fly interstate to visit my parents for a week. I remember being very fretful on those days when I would normally have met him."

"I guess he felt the same."

"Yes, but he never really said. School resumed and we went back to meeting in the café. Months went by. Then I got a text message one night. Late."

"Ooh, what did it say?"

Heather sighed and shifted position. "Something like, *'We must meet tomorrow. Wife and I separating. Will send msg when coming over.'*"

"Wow!"

"Yes, I didn't know whether to laugh or cry. Couldn't sleep."

"How did you feel though?"

"I just wasn't sure how this was going to play out. Did he plan to move in with me and how did I feel about that?"

"So you were confused. With good reason. I can't wait to hear what happened next."

"Neither could I. But I woke the next morning and it was May 13th."

"Oh no!" Meg put her hand over her mouth.

"Oh, yes."

They sat in silence. From the corner of her eye Meg watched Heather, who was staring out a window with tears coursing down her cheeks. Meg looked at the plans for the school house. She added lines with swift, strong strokes, and all that could be heard was the scratch of the pencil crossing the paper.

"I can see now why you thought he might not have wanted children."

"We never even got to speak about it."

"But look at you now. So many!"

Heather laughed through the tears. "Yes, so many."

CHAPTER TWENTY ONE

Meg was in her bathroom, discovering what a cold sweat really felt like. The package was in her left hand, and she ripped the top off with the right. Holding the device below her, she squatted over the toilet and let the hot stream of her urine run over the end, where indicated. Then she sat down and waited. It wasn't long before the blue line showed up in the window.

"No, no, no, NO!" She screamed. "NO. NO. This can't be!"

Several thoughts passed through her mind almost simultaneously. Could it be a false positive? Was the test kit out of date? Was it really possible to be pregnant after just one night with a very old time-travelling man? Besides, she shouldn't have been fertile—her period had only finished two days before she was with William.

Deep-down, however, she knew it was right and that the reason she had taken the test was because she recognised the symptoms from pre-May 2013, when she'd had three pregnancies.

She sat for some time staring at the blue line, running various scenarios through her mind. Mostly she was afraid. She'd suffered toxaemia three times in three pregnancies, each time worse than the previous one. The last birth was catastrophic, and the child had died. She didn't want this to happen in this strange world where the necessary medical care was clearly unavailable.

Or was it? What if William was there?

A thought came to Meg that restored her sense of humour, and it was so funny that she laughed out loud. She was imagining the normally cool and calm India, and how rattled she'd be by this particular merging of DNA.

On entering the community house, Meg sensed a change in the air. Something was happening. She hurried through to the back and found Heather trying to cope with feeding all the children.

"Oh, hi Meg." She sounded tired. "We were awake early. India's in labour—out in the caravan."

"Why didn't someone come and get me?"

"William said not to. Said to let you sleep."

Meg frowned and trod heavily as she left the house and walked toward the caravan. The door was open, and Meg could hear voices and a baby's cry. "Two beautiful girls, India. Aren't you lucky?" Connie's voice was high and warm.

Meg could hear William talking in his low, soothing voice, explaining something to the new mother. Meg moved in further so she could hear.

"...that technology I was telling you about. Makes everything a lot easier on the mother."

"It was wonderful. So easy."

When Meg entered the room at the end of the caravan where the double bed was, she saw Connie straightening the bedclothes. William was leaning against the door frame, smiling at the new mother and her daughters. India looked no different to normal, except her glasses were on a bench beside the bed. She looked up.

"Meg. Oh, you're here at last!"

"Someone should have fetched me!" She shot a stern look at William.

"No need, lovely girl. Everything went smoothly and India did a sterling job."

India laughed. "William performed some of his special magic. I hardly felt a thing."

"Nevertheless, you'll need some rest now. Do you want us to take the babies?"

"No, thanks William. They'll be fine here. Come and

talk to me Meg."

William shuffled out of the tiny room, and Meg took his place. India patted the bed, and the other woman sat on the edge. "You've got no idea how easy that was. Amazing."

"I wonder how his magic would work with severe toxaemia, you know, like Connie's birth."

"Oh, I've got an idea that he can fix most things with his bag of tricks."

Meg almost told her then—the news of the pregnancy—but felt this wasn't the time. This was India's special day.

George was offering her the bottle, talking about how it was the perfect accompaniment to the special pasta dish he'd just served. Sunday nights had become special—pastas and other delicacies, served with specially matched wines. This was a Chianti from the Tuscan region, the black rooster on the label proving the authenticity of the bottle.

Meg felt herself turning green at the very thought of alcohol, and shook her head violently. "No thanks George. I've gone off it a bit." Besides, the last time she'd indulged was the night she spent with William and look where that had gotten her.

She'd waited for William to approach her again, feeling

certain he'd want more of the pleasures he'd enjoyed so thoroughly. She'd even thought they might become a 'couple'. After several weeks of watching him carefully, and trying to read his mood, she'd finally said something.

She'd found him alone in the shed, sitting at a bench and looking at slides that he'd pass under the microscope. As she'd entered, he hadn't looked up, but said, "Ah, the lovely Meg. To what do I owe this visit?"

"It's been a while since we had a talk. I thought I'd come and hang out here for a few minutes."

"Certainly, dear girl. Pull up a chair and I'll finish up here."

"No, don't let me disturb you. Keep working. What are you looking at?"

"Nothing exciting—just testing the quality of the water being held in the tanks."

"And?"

"It's excellent." He sat back with satisfaction. "You're looking good. Very healthy."

"Thanks, William. You're looking pretty good yourself." She took a deep breath. "I was wondering..."

"Yes?"

"You enjoyed our night together, right?"

William had thrown his head back and laughed. "You

know the answer to that, Meg." He'd looked at her face, searchingly. "Ah, I see. You're wondering why I haven't been back for more."

"Well, I did wonder..."

"For two reasons, Meg. The first is that it would be stupid for me to form any liaisons in this place and time. Our night together really shouldn't have happened. I'm meant to hide away and not cause any changes."

"That's why you lived out in the desert."

"Yes. I shouldn't be here among you and certainly shouldn't make love to a beautiful woman."

"And the second reason?"

"It's just not what we do, Meg. We don't allow ourselves that incredible range of emotion, and I can see why. You really rocked my little boat there for a while."

"How do you mean?"

"Naturally, I wanted more. I felt like I was losing control. I could see us setting up a home together. I felt..." He'd wiped his forehead with the back of his hand. "I can't do these things, Meg. I'm not made of that sort of stuff. I was losing control."

"That's what happens, William."

"What—you're saying it's not just me?"

"We fall in love. We feel moments of incredible joy and

then deep despair. It's what makes us human."

"You felt it too—with me?"

"Yes."

William had exhaled loudly. "I can't stay here, Meg. The time will come all too soon when I'll have to go."

"With regret, I hope."

"Huge regret and some mind-blowing memories. Wait until I tell Martin." He'd stopped suddenly and his face reddened. "I suppose it wouldn't be gentlemanly to tell Martin..."

Meg had laughed. "Tell him all you want. Make him very jealous."

"What a wonderful woman you are, Meg. I'm going to miss you so much. I've been so lucky to know you."

Now, as she sat at the fully-laden table and watched the happiness of those around her, she felt alone and isolated. She was in a mess, her pregnancy still a secret, and she didn't know where to turn. She pushed the feeling away and smiled bravely. One thing she knew for sure—since she'd had to survive in this new world—she was strong and could handle whatever was thrown at her. She'd be all right.

"I'm afraid I just lack something when it comes to breastfeeding." India sighed and disengaged her daughter, who immediately began the terrible cry of hunger. "I hope Heather and Connie can help out."

She passed the infant to Meg and buttoned her shirt up. She lifted the second twin into her own arms and the two women began walking toward the house.

"I'm not a good mother, Meg."

"Nonsense."

"No, I'm really not. I know I'm not. When the children aren't around I just sort of forget about them."

"I wouldn't worry too much. We're all a bit different. Heather and Connie have enough mothering in them for all the children."

"Yes. They did promise to raise these girls if I had more. I'll try my best on my own first." She patted the baby on the back. "One day I'll check the DNA of these two."

"Two? Oh, the babies?"

"Yeah, it's puzzling. I don't actually know how I got pregnant."

"We all thought it was John—just before he died."

"Well, originally I thought there was a chance of that, but the facts don't lie."

"So?"

"I don't know. One day I'll run the tests."

"Speaking of babies..."

"Hmm?"

Meg stopped and looked squarely at India. "I have some news."

"Oh?"

"But it's just between the two of us for now, okay?"

"Sure."

"Now I'm pregnant."

India blinked slowly. "Are you sure?"

"Yes."

"But who?"

"William."

"Oh my God, Meg. No. No. That can't be! No! Good God. Think of the genes!"

"I thought it might rattle your cage a bit."

"It can't be!"

"Do you think I should terminate it?"

India looked shocked for a moment, then raised her brows.

"How many weeks?"

"Between seven and eight."

"We'll have to make a decision quickly. I've already got William's DNA sequence. I'll get a sample from you. I'll try and do some modelling—I don't really want to go back to UQ." She handed the baby to Meg absently, and began moving toward her shed with a determined step.

Meg smiled and looked down at the twins. "I'm afraid your mother has bigger fish to fry." She'd have to go inside and ask Connie and Heather if it was possible for each of them to start breast-feeding an extra baby.

The scene at Meg's house was subdued. India and Meg faced William who sat across the dining table from them. The table was empty—this was not a celebration.

"All right, lovely ladies. What do we need to discuss? Why the long faces?"

India looked at Meg, who cleared her throat. She noticed, almost absently, that her hands were shaking.

"I'm pregnant!" Her eyes filled with hot tears. This caused a flashback to the last time she told a man that news— her mostly-absent photographer boyfriend who had taken the news very badly. She hadn't seen him again until the night of May 13th, 2013 when she found him lying dead in her best friend's bed.

William's face was a picture of shock—the women witnessed all the blood draining from it. He seemed to age another ten years in those few moments. "No. This cannot be."

"Well it is." India was in no-nonsense mode. "We need

to forget about the emotional aspect of this situation and consider the scientific side."

Williams mouth was opening and closing like a dying fish. Meg became alarmed. She covered his hand with her own and squeezed it. "It's okay, William. We'll work something out."

"There are several angles to consider." India consulted her notes. "Firstly, the effect of this situation on the ongoing human population. Then there's the possibility of termination —is this the better and safer option? Thirdly, that Meg has a history of severe toxaemia which makes her pregnancies a huge health risk, even with modern medical intervention."

"I conceived a child. Just like that?"

"Yes, William. You're a legend, but you're not listening to me."

"It would be my child. I could raise it like a father?"

India and Meg looked puzzled. "How are children raised in your time?" asked the scientist.

"Well, conception takes place in vitro. The embryo is planted in a woman, a woman chosen for her capacity to carry the child. This all takes place separately."

"And when the child is born?"

"Well, you see—we don't know the child. Our sperm is harvested when needed and put through various processes.

We are remote from the whole event."

"So, how did you know what to do at India's birth?"

"Oh, I attended many births at the facility where they took place. I considered myself a scientist and wanted to learn how it worked. I became quite an expert."

"But you never knew which children were yours?"

"I never knew if I even fathered any. My sperm may not have been suitable."

"No wonder you're excited at this news, then." India frowned. "But it doesn't mean it's a good idea."

"Tell me what you know."

India launched into a lecture on the research she'd been working feverishly on for the past forty-eight hours. Meg, not understanding the technology, let her mind drift. She stood and looked over the Glasshouse Mountains to the coast, not really seeing anything. Finally India turned the last page of her notes and stopped talking.

William looked grave. "This is exactly why it is a terrible idea for time-travellers to mix with the population."

"It's still early enough to perform a very low-risk termination."

"But it's my child!"

"It could kill Meg. Especially if you aren't here to help with the birth."

"This decision cannot be taken lightly!" William's mouth was set in a straight line.

"Of course not. That's why I've been working so hard on it." India was sounding frustrated.

"Whatever we decide now will cause an immediate effect back in my own time, for the good or bad, and really we're not sure which it will be, for all your modelling."

"True."

"But you're saying it's a big risk, genetically speaking."

"Yes."

William sighed. "Give me all your research and two days to look at it." He looked to where Meg was standing by the window with her back to them. Right then she seemed so defenceless. "What do you think, darling Meg?"

She turned and they could see the tears streaming down her face. "I'm grateful that you want this child, William. I'm glad you didn't want to get rid of it without further thought. I find I've grown very fond of you and have decided that, if you want to take the risk, I will too. As long as you are here at the birth."

India shook her head in irritation. "No, no, no. Emotion must not play a part in this. It just can't."

Meg and William were oblivious to her words. They were gazing at each other as though under a spell. William rose and took Meg's hand. He leaned forward and kissed her on the lips. "To think we silly humans of the future are denying ourselves so much *life.*"

"Tell me, William. Tell me again how you'll make sure you're back for the birth."

William's smile was indulgent and gentle. "Of course, my lovely lady. How could I stay away?"

Three of them—Meg, William and India—were standing in the increasing desert heat of central Queensland. They were at the top of Mt Walker, west of Hughenden. The tiny outback hospital could be seen in the distance.

"So you're not worried about that thing you were telling us." India swatted a fly. "About how many times you can return."

Meg frowned. "Yes! I remember now, you telling me— back when we first met—that this might possibly have been your last visit."

"Only possibly."

"But—"

"You girls must go now. It's a long drive home and I don't know how much longer it will be before I can be transported."

Meg looked at India. The other woman shrugged.

"I don't like this. It feels like you're running away." Meg looked at William with welling eyes.

"No, I'm not your bad-boy photographer or cheating ex-husband. I was happy to find out I'm going to be a father, remember? Don't go silly on me, Meg. You're stronger than that."

India put her arm around Meg in a rare gesture of affection. "It'll be okay."

Meg nodded and wiped her eyes with a sleeve. "Sorry. Hormones."

"But you're sure they're going to pick you up?" India looked around the empty desert.

"Yes, certain. Then I'll find out how to make my food and I'll take care of some other details. When I return it will be with more medical equipment and some more technological toys for you, India."

The scientist rubbed her hands together. "I can't wait."

William turned back to Meg and placed a hand on her swelling belly. "Know that I'll be back. Know that if I'm not back it was because of things that are out of my control."

Meg paled. "But...."

"There's always an element of risk."

"I wish you could just stay!"

"I'd starve to death. You wouldn't want that."

"No, I wouldn't."

"Go now, my sweet." He kissed her gently again. "Know that every second I'm away from you will hurt me here." He placed his hand over his chest. "How unscientific is that, India?"

"Very, William—but very romantic."

The women moved to Meg's car, their reluctance showing in the way they walked. Once the engine was running, Meg felt better. It was time to go home.

CHAPTER TWENTY TWO

Connie's outline moved behind the section of frosted glass set into the front door. Meg could see two smaller figures, dancing around her.

As the door swung inwards, Connie began speaking rapidly in the breathless way she always spoke. Two figures hurtled past her, shouting and drowning out her words. "Meg, Meg!"

"Hello Maisie. Hello Thomas. How are you both today?" They ignored the question and ran through to the living area, crying in delight at the view of the mountains.

"Sorry to disturb you, Meg."

"It's fine. What's up?"

"Oh, I just wanted to have a talk. Can I come in?"

"Ah, yes. Sorry." Meg stood back from the door and let the young woman through.

"Mum, Mum. Look!"

Connie joined the twins at the window and agreed that the view was wonderful. She took some books from her bag and suggested that the two of them sit quietly and look at them while she and Meg talked.

"There, that might work for a few minutes."

"Did the others send you to talk to me?"

"No, not really. We're all worried about you, though. I know India comes and visits you sometimes, but the rest of us…"

"I'm just not feeling very social right now."

"Okay, but you can't spend your whole pregnancy isolated and angry like this."

"Can't I?"

"No. It's not good."

"Look—"

"Perhaps if you explain why you're so upset."

"No offence, but I'm not sure it's any of your business."

Connie looked like she had been slapped. Tears came to her eyes.

Meg looked at the younger woman for a few seconds. Then the words began to come in a torrent. "Because I was tricked! I was tricked into having this baby and I'm just…" She took a deep breath. "Just—*really angry.*"

"But I don't understand."

"Oh you don't, eh? Okay I'll tell you. It took me a long

time to work it all out, but now I know for sure."

Connie was looking bewildered.

"It wasn't until William left that I could see it so clearly. He's a clever man. Too clever."

"What did he do exactly?" Connie blushed. "I mean—to make you angry like this?"

"The signs were there, but I was blind to them. You see, when he first got here, he told us about the portal closing and how this trip was possibly his last, but when he and I got involved, I forgot all about that. Went into denial. Believed his stories—"

"What stories?"

"They came later. First, he manipulated me somehow. Made me act in a way I would never normally. Made me seduce him, so that it didn't appear that he was at fault."

"I see..." Connie looked doubtful.

"I've got a thing about that, about being the one to make the first move to a man. I just don't do it, never have, never will. I'd had a couple of wines, but that wasn't enough to explain my actions. I think he planned all this out—a new experiment. Just one more before he went home forever. Get me pregnant. See what effect the merging of our DNA would have in the future."

"Oh!"

"Like the Bill and Ben experiment. He cloned those two and look at how that turned out."

"That was sad."

"So he got me to seduce him and somehow tricked my body into releasing an egg before it was due. I reckon he knew I was pregnant almost immediately." Meg frowned and looked at her forearm. "The microchip! That's how he knew!" She strode into the kitchen. Connie was diverted by the children asking a question. By the time she joined Meg, the other woman was running the blade of a sharp knife through a flame being thrown from a lighter.

"Oh, no!"

Meg took a deep breath and placed the knife against the skin of her left forearm. Connie put a hand over her mouth and looked away. The knife sliced cleanly and Meg used the sharp tip to dig around in the wound until the chip came free. "Got you, you bastard!" She held the bloody arm over the sink while fishing in a drawer for dressings. "Fix me up will you?"

Connie was feeling faint, but helped Meg dress the wound.

"So then all the acting began—shock at hearing the news of the pregnancy, excitement at the idea of being a father, promising to be here for the birth—I reckon he waited here just long enough to make sure I'd go through with the pregnancy before he left."

"You're not sure of any of this, Meg."

"Oh, I think I am."

"Well, even if he did, you only have one baby in there. I reckon he would have made certain of that." She began warming to the theme. "You know, he might have done something to you with those gadgets of his to make sure you won't have any childbirth problems."

"Maybe. Maybe not. But he tricked me and manipulated me and let me tell you, I'm as angry as a cut snake."

"Okay. You're angry, but that's not helping anyone, least of all you. I think you have to let go of all that negative energy now."

"Oh, you do, do you?" Meg's tone was sarcastic. "Who are you to tell me—?"

"Your friend, and I'm not going to let you drive me away. We all miss you. The kids miss you. We're also finding it tough without your help."

Meg stood in the centre of the kitchen, holding the wound tightly through the dressings. "I'm just so sick of these bastards—these men that have used me and then dumped me. This is the third one now. Three out of three. Quite a record."

Connie sensed that some of the anger was dissipating. "Just come for dinner tonight. I'll make sure George cooks something special. Please?"

Meg was silent for a moment. "Well, okay, but that's all I'm promising."

Connie smiled and clapped. "Meg's coming to dinner tonight, kids!"

"Yay! Yay!"

The young woman bundled the children into the car, and then Meg could hear her driving slowly down to the road. She saw the bloody microchip sitting on the bench and snatched it up grimly. In the bathroom, she threw it into the toilet bowl and, for the first time in recent memory, smiled as she witnessed it going to a watery grave.

Another terrible spasm racked Meg's body. She raised herself off the pillows and let out a primal scream.

"That's good, Meg." India's voice was soft and soothing. "You're doing well. Don't push again just yet."

"Easy for you to say," Meg said through clenched teeth. "You got the easy birth."

"Hush and concentrate. Take those short breaths. Puff, puff, puff."

Meg mimicked the other woman's breathing. She tried to focus on positives. At least there was only one child to push out.

"Now—a big push. Go for it, Meg. It's time to meet your child."

Meg bore down with all her strength. If it didn't come out this time, it could damn well stay there as far as she was concerned. She was over it.

"Here we go. Ah, wonderful! A little boy!"

The baby gave a lusty cry without having to be prompted. India laid him on Meg's belly and covered both of them with a sheet. "I'll just take your blood pressure, but I don't expect any problems." She wrapped the band around Meg's arm and pumped the black bag with her left hand and then released the valve. "Perfect. You were lucky this time."

"I'm not sure about lucky—but I'm alive at least."

"Think of the positives."

Meg snorted. Even though she hadn't expected William to return, a part of her had still held hope. Now she knew she had been justified in her anger.

India cut the umbilical cord and massaged Meg's lower abdomen until the afterbirth was produced. She lifted the baby off Meg, and wrapped him tightly before returning him to her arms. The child opened his eyes and regarded Meg very seriously.

"Look, India," Meg whispered. "Look at his eyes."

Both woman stared with rapt attention into the green/blue/violet depths of the child's irises. His eyes were notable on two counts. It wasn't just the colour, it was the incredible intelligence that shone from them.

"Wow." India's voice was a whisper. "He's going to be very special, you know. I can see it from the DNA modelling."

Meg smiled and touched the boy's damp hair. "Oh, he'll be special all right. And you never know, one day he might be able to tell me what the hell happened to his father."

India leaned over the edge of the mezzanine. "Connie! Come and meet the newest member of our community!"

The young woman's footsteps clattered on the stairs. She arrived, breathless. "Ooh, isn't he lovely! Look at those eyes!"

India began cleaning up the mess from the birth. She gathered an armful of linen and towels, and took them downstairs.

Connie smiled and pushed some curls from Meg's forehead. "You did well. I knew you would. And now you have a beautiful baby boy to make your life special."

Meg nodded. "I guess you're right."

"Cuppa?"

"That's the thing about you, Connie. You're always good for a strong tea after childbirth. Yes, I'd love one."

Night was falling, and Meg looked over the edge of the mezzanine to the mountains and beyond. There was no wind and the world looked to have a special stillness about it. As she watched, the mountains began turning pink and then orange. She began to relax and her breathing slowed.

A new sensation washed over her, a feeling of peace and contentment. She could feel it seeping into her body and her soul. It took her by surprise but it was beautiful.

The baby moved his head and yawned. He looked back into Meg's eyes and contemplated her seriously.

Meg smiled and touched his cheek. The anger and disappointment was fading further, and she began feeling light and contented. All the pieces had fallen into place for her. She now understood the events that led to that moment and why they happened in the way they did.

The baby yawned again and fell asleep. Meg smiled and relaxed further into the pillows. Then another feeling seeped into her and she felt it embrace her like a warm cloak. It was a sense of having put down roots in this world, and for the first time since May 2013, she felt she was where she was meant to be. It was something new, something she had never felt before in this strange new world. It was almost like a sense of belonging. Yes, that was it.

She was now exactly where she belonged.

The third book in the "Strange Worlds" series will be published in 2015.

If you would like to be advised when it becomes available, simply email: birdcallpublishing@gmail.com

The 'Brenda Cheers – Author' Facebook page will also provide this information. 'LIKE' the page to receive updates.

Thank you for reading "In a Time Where They Belong". If you enjoyed it, please consider telling your friends or posting a short review. Word of mouth is an author's best friend and much appreciated.

Thank you.

Birdcall Publishing

ACKNOWLEDGEMENTS

While researching the genome sequencing scenes of this book, I discovered how helpful and friendly some of the members of the scientific community can be. I would like to thank the following scientists for their advice: Robyn Mansfield, Chris McKenzie, Ken McGrath and (especially) John Stephen. My gratitude is enormous.

My team of beta-readers are special people who give me the sort of sturdy advice that all writers need. Thank you Rebecca, Tez, Robyn, Tracey and Mum.

I must also thank Laura Kenny. You possess knowledge that I lack and I appreciate being able to call on you for advice. Thank you.

ABOUT THE AUTHOR

Brenda Cheers is a writer of both short and long fiction.
She lives in Brisbane, Australia with her partner and two daughters.
See more at www.brendacheersbooks.com